HATE JACKET

M. Andrew Patterson

ISBN-13: 978-1-7346014-0-4

To Steve.
Who taught me that not all fathers are monsters

Acknowledgments

This novel took eight tries to get right and it wouldn't have been possible without the love and support of so many people. Know that if you don't find your name here, it was because I couldn't fit everyone on one page. First and foremost, thanks go to my wife Jessica who helped me make this all possible. She gave me the push to take the chance on self-publishing. Her love and support are more than I could have ever expected. I would also like to thank my children: Alex, Nathan, Joseph, Gracelyn, Ben, and Theo. You guys are rock stars and I love you all so much. To my mom who putting up with me as a child. To Steve who was more of a father than I expected. Thank you to my cat, Lili, who has used my lap as a bed for the duration of writing this novel. All the thanks to my critique partner, Bonnie without whom I would have probably given up a long time ago. Thank you to Star who got me started on this crazy journey and reminds me to always "Breath Dammit!" I would also like to thank the many readers who have provided feedback including K.T., Jaime, Shelby, Ayah, Ada, Sheryl, anyone else who ever dared to read even part of a draft. Finally, huge thanks go to my editor, Kaelan at Chimera Edits, who helped me get this the way Julius wanted it.

Author's Note

Due to the nature of this book, I felt it best if I made note of potentially harmful content. The following is a list of that content. I did my best to be respectful and appropriate in my depictions. Some of it was drawn from my own experiences and some is purely fictional. This book wasn't an easy book to write, but one that I felt needed to write.

- Alcoholism
- Bullying
- Child Abuse
- Depression
- Discussions of molestation
- Discussions of self-harm
- Kidnapping
- Indications of rape
- Suicidal attempt and discussions of suicide

CHAPTER ONE

I should have my own chair in here with bright neon letters that say, "This seat belongs to Julius Monroe, Wellsville High's number one fuck up."

Ms. Stevens—Sorry, Dr. Stevens, vice-principal extraordinaire —stares at me with her usual bitchy, disapproving look. Word has it she was supposed to be the principal. Guess the good 'ol boys found someone they liked better and now she's stuck at the bottom of the heap. She takes it out on me, her favorite school loser, and anyone else with the misfortune of screwing up.

She stops talking and glares at me. I'm not paying attention and she knows it. The lines around her mouth deepen.

"What?" I ask in my best I don't give a damn voice.

If I push it enough, I wonder if I'll get a vein to pop out of her head. That would be so awesome. Maybe break up the monotony of staring at the pictures of her kids while she rambles on about appropriate behavior and attire. I could have my ass exposed and my pants around my thighs and nobody would care, but wear a jacket with the word hate on it, and I get yanked into the office and told what a horrible person I am. How dare I wear something so offensive as if the world wasn't horrible enough as it is.

"Mr. Monroe, that jacket is simply unacceptable."

"It's a personal expression."

I try to keep my face calm as she presses her lips into a thin white line. I'm not lying, it is. I can't stand all the hypocrisy around me, so my jacket says it like it is. Life isn't all unicorns and fairy farts. Bad crap happens every day.

Dr. Stevens sighs and pinches the bridge of her nose. "Yes, I get that Julius. However," she pauses dramatically. "There have been several complaints…"

"Yeah, I know. The perfect, happy, popular kids don't like it and because they don't like it, we have to kiss their ass because mommy and daddy are on the school board!"

I hate those jerks, especially their ring leader, Greg Schlesinger. He and his buddies have had it in for me for years. Greg hates me and my jacket which is why I'm here with Dr. Stevens. He wants it, and me, gone. We all know who is really in charge around here and it isn't the good doctor.

I'm not giving up my jacket. I've worked too hard on it. Besides, it's totally badass. After the first time it got damaged by the Monster, I decided to fix it. Needless to say, I sucked, but I guess I'm stubborn because I kept trying to fix it. Eventually it started changing, and as my technique improved, so did the jacket.

I change it up here and there. Add something new, take away something old. It's a patchwork of fabrics. It looks more haphazard than it really is. I considered dyeing it all one color, black, but it just fit that it was so many different colors. Some of the artwork I hand stitched, others I drew with car paint. I wear it, people leave me alone.

"Mr. Monroe…Julius…I understand that you are trying to make a statement, but that jacket is completely inappropriate."

"Yeah, whatever."

"Not whatever. There are safety issues involved."

Oh crap. No, don't say what I think you're gonna say. Not the studs. They're not even sharp. Ok, the ones on the shoulder may be. Dammit. Knew I should have left those off.

"Those studs on your shoulder could cause a lot of damage. The chains are just barely acceptable. I'm going to have to ask you to leave the jacket here and pick it up when you leave for the day."

"Hell no!" I surge to my feet, anger boiling inside me.

"Julius! Sit down!"

I sit. She has that kind of voice. I wait for her to say something, a scowl plastered on my face.

"Now, I can't force you to turn your jacket over to me. I would prefer if you did. It will remain locked in my office until the end of school."

Sure it will, until Greg decides he want it, and then you'll hand it over no questions asked.

"No." I cross my arms and glare.

Dr. Stevens rubs her temples. I'm guessing she's got one hell of a headache going now. Good. She's one of them, more interested in brown-nosing the PTA than doing anything useful. The faster she can get the trash out of the school, the better its reputation. Which ultimately means more money. Go figure.

"Ok." she looks at me, exasperation written across every wrinkle. "You can't wear it until it conforms to the school's dress policy. You either put it in your locker or take it home."

"Locker's broke. I'll take it home." I stand to leave.

"If you go home, I will be forced to suspend you."

I pause. "So."

I should care, but I'm so angry at her. She's pushed me into a corner and I'm not going to wimp out and give in.

Dr. Stevens pulls a few sheets of paper from her desk and picks up a pen.

"Your grades are already in jeopardy. If you miss too many more days, I'll be forced to mark you truant. We've been very lenient with you, Julius."

I snort, eliciting another sigh from the esteemed Dr. Stevens. As I'm heading out, her voice stops me again.

"Julius."

I don't bother to turn. If I look at her, I might crack and give in. I have to be strong and stand up for what's mine. Nobody else will do it.

"We're not the enemy."

I don't say it, but they are. All of them are. I don't bother closing the door as I leave her office. My scowl in place, I keep my head down and avoid eye contact as I head towards the freedom the school doors offer. Outside where I can breathe and not suffocate under the double standards of high school. Problem is, outside of school lurks my father, the Monster.

I'm too busy not looking at anyone that I miss the foot stuck out at the last minute. I stumble forward in an attempt to keep from face planting in front of everyone. My efforts are rewarded with my shoulder banging into the door.

"Oh sorry, man." The voice has a barely hidden sneer to it and I know right away I've been pranked by one of the biggest assholes in the school, Greg Schlesinger.

I give him my best glare. Not that it bothers him. The smirk on his face is evidence enough. I should have seen this coming. The desire to smash his face in with a baseball bat is almost overwhelming and it takes everything I have to turn and walk away. He's won this round, but I'll be back to dirty up his school soon enough.

The sky looms over me when I step outside. Dark, thick, heavy clouds full of rain and fury ready to unleash themselves on me. It's like one of those scenes from a movie where the dejected hero walks away, rain pouring down. I head home, I don't bother hurrying. I know what's coming. The air is like breathing soup it's so humid. Two blocks away from the school, the skies open up. It takes only moments to soak me completely. Good thing I'm not made of sugar, shit, or anything else that might melt in the rain.

Thunder rumbles adding insult to injury of my life. Each one is loud enough that I can't help but jump a little. I'm not scared of thunder per say, but loud noises have always made me jumpy. Not surprising considering who I live with. At least he and his most recent girlfriend are at work. Just thinking about them makes my stomach churn. My life is a series of screwed up crap that go from bad to worse. One of these days I could end up dead and I doubt anybody would really care. Not those two. They're both too wrapped up in whatever BS they have brewing. Their relationship is a powder keg and when, not if, it blows up, I'll be caught in the blast radius.

The slow slosh of tires in the growing river that is the street draws me from my dark thoughts. I don't look directly at it but catch a glimpse of a very recognizable white and red '65 Mustang. I draw my gaze from the high-performance tires up to the driver's side window. Blake, former Wellsville High's darling all-state linebacker and all-around nice guy, waves frantically at me to get in. Somewhere in the mess of my life, I made a friend. Not sure how it happened, but it did. He and his folks are just good people and have kind of been a refuge for me growing up. Their house has always been open to me when I need to get away from my father.

I don't deserve any of it, but I won't say no when it's offered. I'm sure I'm more like that pitiful, ugly, stray puppy on the street corner that looks half-dead that makes you want to take it home. Who cares if I pee on the carpet and have fleas. Right? Ok, not that last bit, but the point is I don't belong anywhere but with my father. I'm a nobody, a nothing. There was a time, long ago, when that wasn't the case. But that was before the Monster took over and destroyed everything. When my mom snuck out in the middle of the night and never looked back leaving me with him.

Blake unlocks the door and I slide into the warm interior. I know I'm ruining the leather on the seats, but Blake doesn't care.

"Stalking me again?" I ask with a lopsided grin to hide the dark thoughts.

His eyes crinkle when he smiles. I swear I hear the sighs of the varsity cheerleading squad. He has that kind of smile. Close-cropped black hair, brown-eyed, tall, all-American good looks. I catch the hint of a tattoo on his dark skin, partially hidden by the white fitted t-shirt. Add the personality of a saint and you have Blake. Life is not fair. I'm a dark smudge of grease next to him. Not that he cares. Like I said, he's good people. Even if he is just helping out the local mangy stray.

"Well, you did look pretty pathetic walking in the rain," he says as he pulls back onto the road as if reading my thoughts.

He doesn't ask why I'm not in school. He doesn't need to. He knows either I'm ditching or I got suspended. He's tried to put me on the straight and narrow before, but it never worked. So he gave up. There's a first for everything.

I give him a flat look. "Thanks."

He smirks as he navigates toward my house. "Well, you're lucky I was out. Dad needed some parts."

Blake's father runs a body shop. I work there when I can. Pays decent for a kid who has no experience with cars. I feel a little bad about taking money after all they do for me, but I'm trying to stash as much as I can with the hopes that I might be able to get the hell out of my dad's. If I'm lucky, I'll have enough to keep me from living in a cardboard box for a month or two.

"Tell him I'll stop by in a couple days and help out." I leave time lines vague and Blake and his dad know it. They know things change rapidly in my life. What they don't know is I don't always know when I'll run into the Monster and end up with a few fresh bruises. Faded ones are easier to hide and explain away.

"Will do," Blake says evenly. He taps his fingers on the steering wheel. It's a nervous action and a definite tell that something is bothering him.

"You ok, man?" I ask to break the tension.

Blake waves a hand dismissively. "Nah. Just random garbage in my head." His eyes flick to me. "You need a place to crash?"

For a moment I want to say yes. Getting away from home with the opportunity to see Brit, Blake's sister, are almost too much to ignore. Correction, Blake's smoking hot sister that is so far out of my league and thinks I'm her brother. That sister.

On top of that, Lela and my father have been arguing a lot. Listening to her sobbing in the bathroom after he's done with her tears holes in me. I don't dare stand up to him. I just pick up the pieces and keep doing the best I can.

Blake's voice jars me out of my thoughts.

"I mean, I know you don't have any clothes at the house, but I bet you can borrow some of Brit's until yours dry." How he says that with a straight face is beyond me.

So I'm not the biggest guy. And so what if his sister is almost my height. I'm not going to let him get away with that one. I might have long hair, but I don't look like a girl.

"I don't know," I say, my finger tapping thoughtfully on my chin. "Those skirts she wears would probably make my butt look big."

Blake just about crashes the car from laughing.

"Jesus, Blake! You're gonna get us both killed!" I grab the JC-handle to add emphasis. I mean, why else would you put a handle near the top of the passenger side door?

"What? You mean like this?" Blake yanks on the wheel, causing the car to drift on the ponding water. I bite back a scream, my knuckles white on the handle. He's pulled stunts like this before. I know better than to make any noise, not that it will distract him, but because any response from me will only add fuel to the fire. Also, I don't want to die. Blake casually rights the car and continues to drive, the tires making rooster tails in the puddles.

Before I'm ready, we're there. My house. It's old, the paint faded and peeling. It used to be beige, but now the color is so dirty it's a faded color somewhere between white and gray. What's left of the yard is rough and overgrown. The mower broke some time ago and my dad's too busy drinking to get it fixed. I could take it to the shop and see if Mr. T could get it running again, but my dad hates the Thompsons.

Blake touches my shoulder. It's light, almost timid. "You gonna be ok?"

I look at him, his face lined with worry. I almost break down and tell him to take me to his house.

"Nah. I'll be fine." I manage a weak smile. Blake isn't fooled, but he lets me go.

"Ok. Call if you need anything," he says as I reach for the door handle.

"Thanks," I say as Blake drops his hand back to the steering wheel.

Blake looks like he's about to say something else, but closes his mouth. We fist bump and I'm out of the safety of the car and into the muggy September afternoon. At least the rain has stopped. Blake waits until I'm at the door before he heads off. I take a deep breath and open it.

"Oh, your home early!" Lela's voice catches me off guard. She isn't home this time of day either.

I grunt noncommittally without bothering to look in her direction and start heading toward my room. I don't want to get into a conversation with her. Especially if my dad isn't home. Things happen when she and I are alone. Her hand catches my sleeve halting me. My blood freezes at the touch.

"You poor dear! You're all wet!" Her voice oozes with honeyed sweetness that pools in my stomach in a caustic mix of fear and shame.

My eyes betray me and are drawn to her face. I don't see the yellowing bruise on her cheek or the slight puffiness at the corner of her lips, all I see is the burning in her eyes. My blood freezes as she raises her hand and runs her finger down my jaw.

CHAPTER TWO

We stand there, frozen. Her red-painted nails pressed into my skin ever so gently, but each one is like a spike through me. A razor cutting my flesh and exposing my soul. The heat in her dark eyes cools my body into stone. With anyone else, I would be on fire. Not her. Not Lela. I know what she wants and I want to give in. But I can't. It's wrong. She knows it. I know it.

Her fingers fall from my face. She closes her eyes, releasing me from her spell. Her delicate shoulders rise and fall beneath the thin cotton of her shirt and I'm mesmerized by the movement. My eyes trail downward, traitorous. I hate myself for it, but I can't close my eyes or I'll remember that her skin smells like vanilla with a hint of musk that I can only imagine is from being with my father.

The beginnings of tears form in her lashes and I know if they fall, I will go to her. Comfort her. Be what she needs me to be even as I hate myself for it.

She puts her hand against my chest, her fingers hot against my skin. She doesn't push me away or pull me toward her. She just leans there a moment as she fights something within her. I watch her face with its smooth olive skin that she claims is from an Asian grandparent. Minus their usual color, her lips are still full and inviting. I can see why my father was drawn to her. She's like a doll, delicate yet with a quiet strength that my father's brutish mentality would never understand.

"I have to leave," she says, her voice quavering.

She still hasn't opened her eyes. Maybe she's afraid to look at me. Afraid of what emotions flit across my face when I look at her. I try to hide them, but I've never been good at hiding things. Especially not from her.

I still haven't found my voice. My throat is dry from being so close to her. I swallow past the lump. I know what she's saying. She is leaving my father. Leaving me. I don't have the words to ask her to stay. She has to go. We've known that for some time. In the stolen moments of quiet after my father has fallen asleep. In the morning, with the coffee brewing and my father crashing around the house in a desperate attempt to make it to work on time.

I knew it was temporary when she moved in, full of joy and excitement. Then as the fighting escalated and my father's fists bruised her body, she sought me out for comfort. And now she's leaving.

"I didn't see your car out front," I manage to say, the words grating against my barren throat.

She smiles slightly, just an upturn of the lips before they fall again. She takes another shuddering breath before opening her eyes again. The tears are there, but they don't fall.

"It's parked out back. I...I didn't want to have to deal with your father if he came home before I was gone." The words rush out and then the tears fall. I do what I want and hate and pull her close. Her tears mix with the water saturating my clothes. She wraps her arms around me pressing her hands against my back her fingers touching the skin just under the waistline of my jeans. I suppress a shudder and she begs forgiveness in choking sobs.

I stroke her hair and whisper soothing words as she fills my nose with her scent. This time the slight hint of musk is missing, scrubbed from her body. He has no claim on her anymore.

"Come with me," she mumbles into my shirt.

My hand stills and the words choke me.

Lela pulls back and gazes up at me, her eyes pleading. "Please. Come with me."

I shake my head, not trusting the words. If I open my mouth, I'm scared I'll say yes. Going with her won't save me from him. He would follow me. Find me like every other time I've tried to leave.

Besides, I'd be trading one monster for another. Or maybe I'll become the monster. I know it's there, lurking beneath the surface. Waiting for me to let it go. If I'm here, my father can't hurt her again. She'll be free of him and I'll be free of her.

"Tell me no, Julius," her eyes bore into me, daring me to speak, to deny her.

I shake my head and try to pull away, but her fingers are locked at the small of my back. I'm trapped, her body pressing against me. If I try to pry her fingers apart, I might hurt her. As scared as I am, I won't resort to that. I can't. I won't become like him.

"You've never been able to say no before." Her words beat against me. "Come with me. I'll be good to you. We'll be good to each other."

"Please," I beg, panic swallowing my voice. I can't go. It's a mantra in my head as my will crumbles.

"It'll just be you and me," she says, her hands caressing my back, her nails lightly scratching my skin. "You won't have to worry about him anymore. Neither of us will."

I fight against the rising tide of emotions that fight for dominance in my head. Fear twists my gut while anger burns through my veins. Shame stifles them all as desire shoots electricity through my body. I have to stop her. I don't want to stop her. She loves me.

My heart is slamming against my ribs. All it will take is one tiny word. I want to say it, but I'm scared. Scared of what it'll mean. She raises up on her toes, her mouth inches from mine, her eyes blazing.

"No," I choke out just as our lips touch.

But she doesn't stop. She never does.

The shower does nothing to wash the shame from my body. No

matter how hard I scrub, it never goes away. I pretend that I'm not crying despite the hot tears on my face. She's gone and I don't know if I'm happy or sad. All I feel is empty. Nothing. A void. My movements are mechanical as I dress in clean clothes. The old ones smell like her and touching them makes me nauseous. I wrap them in a towel and shove the lot into my laundry basket.

I know I should do something now that Lela is gone, but I don't. I sit there waiting. Waiting for my father to come home. Waiting for the violence to happen. Even though I had nothing to do with it, I'll get the blame. I always do. And maybe I am to blame in some way. Maybe I could have convinced her to stay, sacrificed myself for my father. It's what I'm supposed to do. What I have done for years. Leaving would mean I would be sacrificing myself for her. Difference is, my father loves me.

The door slamming breaks me out of my trance. I've been sitting in the same spot for hours. It felt like minutes. His boots echoes through the house, loud and angry. I should have locked myself in my room. He pauses behind me for a moment and I wait for the inevitable. I don't move, my shoulders slightly hunched. Instead his footsteps retreat towards the bedroom. The air is tense, heavy with the potential. As soon as he sees the room and her stuff missing, he'll rage.

"She's gone," my mouth moves without thinking, the words tumbling onto the floor.

My father pauses. The silence deafening. I wait for him to speak, to act. For a moment I wonder.

His roar shatters the silence, filling the house with primal rage. The whole house shakes with it. I try to stay silent and still like the little mouse that I am. I don't look. I squeeze my eyes shut and grip the couch so hard my knuckles crack.

He rages a moment, breaking and smashing everything in reach, and then it's silent except for my pounding heart and his heavy breathing. He stomps off into his bedroom and I let out a shaky breath. I've survived, but still I don't move.

He always freaks when someone leaves, but usually they've only been here a couple months tops. Lela has been here two years. It wasn't long after I found her on the bathroom floor, crying, her face bloody and bruised. I helped her clean up and after that night, she came to me, confiding and seeking comfort. If I hadn't helped her, maybe she would have left sooner.

I expected his blowup to be bigger. A part of me wants it to be bigger. I did something horrible and deserve whatever is coming to me. I can't help feeling this is because of me. She left because of me.

My father stomps back in, the floor quivering under the assault. His hand clamps down on the back of my jacket and hauls me over the back of the couch. He's completely silent through the whole process. I don't even fight him. I know what's happening next.

He slams me into the wall and shoves a piece of paper in my face.

"What. The Fuck. Is This?!" he screams into my face.

His arm is wedged under my chin, forcing my head back. I try to push his arm away, but it is like trying to move a boulder. I gasp for air and his eyes burn with a cold rage, his face dark red. The veins in his neck throb. I can see the muscles in his arm move as he crumples the paper in his fist.

"You fucking helped her?"

I want to tell him I didn't, but I can't speak. Even if his arm wasn't crushing my throat, I don't think I would have said anything. Words mean nothing to him when he's like this. The Monster is in control. Nothing I say or do will change that. Not for the first time, I wonder if I'm going to die. It wouldn't take much. Just a sharp push and it would be all over. Despite the futility, I still fight his arm, fight to breathe, fight to survive.

He pulls his arm away and I drop the few inches to the ground. Sweet air fills my lungs. The world turns white when he back-fists me, his large class ring digging into my cheek. Blood fills my mouth and I stagger to the floor. The world tilts and spins. He's not done with me though as his steel-toed boot slams into my rib cage driving the breath from my lungs, my ribs shuddering with the impact. I curl into a ball protecting my face and stomach. He screams incoherently and delivers a couple more swift kicks, each one harder than the last.

My own monster wants me to fight, to rage against him. Tear, claw, bite, anything to show him I'm not weak. I push it down. Lock it away in a dark place where it can't escape. I'm too weak and he's too strong. I would lose. The monster inside fights me. It doesn't care. It wants blood. It doesn't care if it is mine. My body trembles with fear and adrenaline as I struggle against it, eventually smothering the blazing inferno until it is nothing but a smoldering rock.

His strong hands tear my jacket as he heaves me up. Somehow, I manage to keep my arms in front of my face as he punches the side of my head. Stars explode behind my eye. His ring cuts me behind my ear and blood runs down my neck, soaking into the collar of my jacket.

His hands are so strong, his arms so powerful, the shock of each hit rattles my teeth. The world grows dark around the edges. I'm going to die. My father is going to kill me. For real this time. I should have left with Lela. He grabs my shoulders and slams me against the wall, denting the sheet-rock. My legs give out and I fall in a heap on the floor.

"You will never, EVER, do this again or I swear to God I will kill you!" He roars at me, inches from my face. "Do you understand me?"

I half nod, unable to do more. The world tilts as he picks me up by my arms and roughly shoves me toward the stairs.

"Now get your sorry ass upstairs. I don't want to fucking see you!"

I stumble away and manage to get up to the stairs without falling. Blood drips from my mouth and behind my ear. The bathroom looms ahead of me. I don't want to see what damage he's done to me. I just want to curl up and sleep, but I can't keep bleeding everywhere.

The harsh light from the bathroom pierces my eyes. I should have left with Lela. My eyes burn, but I refuse to cry. We both made our choices.

CHAPTER THREE

Blood swirls down the drain as I wash out the cut on my cheek. It's shallow, but I'm going to have to find some excuse for it or people might get nosy. Especially the Thompsons. Blake might be my friend, but he's also a very protective friend. If I don't figure out a story before I see him again, he's likely to go try and take on my dad. Blake might be strong, but he's no fighter. My dad fights dirty.

When I was younger, my dad took me to the bar to play pool. Guess he wanted to show me what it was to be a man or something. I remember sitting on a ratty, smelly stool with one leg a little shorter than the others. Every time I shifted my weight, it would clunk and almost topple me off. The air was hazy with cigarette smoke and alcohol.

My dad made good money that night. He had a knack of sniffing out the new guys. People who didn't know he was good. He'd pretend to not know much and then after the first shot, he'd wipe the floor with them. I was in awe. The whole time I'd sit there, a coke in my hand while my dad downed beers and made money.

That was, until he got caught. The guy was huge. Outweighed my father by a good hundred pounds. Tattoos snaked up his arms and his belly strained against his wife-beater. The only hair on his head was the full beard hanging off his chin. He looked mean, but my dad just smiled and the guy fell under his spell.

Until my dad started dropping balls left and right. The guy's face got redder and a large vein started pulsing on his temple. I just stared and kept my mouth shut. That was my job and I didn't want to make my father mad at me. The match devolved into shouting. The large man reared back, his fist raised. Everything slowed down. I opened my mouth to scream a warning, but my dad was faster.

The pool cue slammed between the man's legs, dropping him to his knees. Once his head was bowed in pain, my dad swung the cue like a bat and broke it over the guy's head. The bouncer tackled my father before he could hit the guy again. As it was, blood pooled on the floor mixing with the dirt and grime.

Thankfully the guy lived, but my dad was banned from ever coming back. He was pretty mad when they kicked us out. He screamed and cussed all the way home. I sat in the back, my legs squeezed tight together because I had forgotten to pee before we left.

I gently probe the knot forming behind my ear. Each gentle touch sends a hot spike through my head. I need to put some ice on it, but I'm stuck up here until my dad either crashes or goes out. As pissed as he is, he'll probably hit the bar and blow off some steam. Besides using me for a punching bag, it's his favorite past-time.

I look like hell. Drawn, pale, bruised, and to top it all off, my jacket is torn. Not the first time and I doubt it will be the last. The thing has been through a lot, and like me it's been patched up more times than I can count.

The TV is blaring when I creep out the bathroom. My father might not be able to hear anything over the noise of whatever he's watching, but I don't want to take the chance. Last thing I need is for him to remember I exist.

I slip into my room and lock the door behind me. It's where I should have been instead of being all whiny and depressed on the couch. Maybe he would have wasted his rage on the door instead of me.

The house is old enough, the door isn't one of those hollow

pieces of crap you get at the hardware store. This one's solid and with the lock I've installed, my dad would have to be really determined to get in. It's still possible which is why the dresser is close to the door. Still, like any other defense, it has its limits.

Kind of sad that I have an escape route from my house that has nothing to do with fire safety. Most kids just run to the neighbors. I just run, after jumping from a second story window and praying I don't break anything in the process.

I kick a few dirty clothes out of the way, stripping my jacket off and tossing it onto my small bed. With a pained grunt I drag an old army footlocker from under my bed. Old, battered, and tough as nails, it holds everything I could possibly need to fix my jacket. Buttons, thread, needles, scraps of cloth, you name it.

Started a few years back when my father bought me the original jacket and then promptly tore it a couple days later after a drunken rage. Instead of throwing it away, I kept the jacket figuring I would find someone to fix it or at least show me how. Then one day, up in the attic with all the other forgotten things, I found an old sewing box full of pins and thread.

After a quick look on the Internet and a few good YouTube videos, I was able to fix my jacket. I knew I'd never be able to make it look like it did, so I made a few alterations. Over time, it morphed from a simple jean jacket to a hate spewing, student council pissing off, get me kicked out of school kind of jacket.

Blake rolled his eyes when he saw it, but my dad didn't even notice. I loved it.

The seam ripper makes short work of the threads holding the spiked shoulder panels in place. They're what started all this nonsense, and getting rid of them eases some of the pain lodged in my chest. Grabbing some random pieces from the sewing box, I go to work rebuilding what I had just undone. The bright crimson swatches stand out like a badge of some kind. On a whim, I turn them into military bars across the shoulder. Life's a war and I should look the part.

Once I get those finished, I take a look at the damage my father did. Thankfully, it isn't worse. Just a few broken threads on the sleeve. Gives me a chance to fix the stitching from the last time I jacked with the arm. I'm so focused, I don't notice I've stuck a pin in my finger until I see blood. More blood to mix with what's already on there from earlier. Fitting. With a growl, I keep sewing, letting my blood christen the new stitches.

When I'm sewing, I forget the world. Forget the pain and anger. I pour it all into the jacket where it churns and boils in hateful impotence. People hate it, hate me, because it doesn't hide the pain. It slams them in the face when I walk down the hall. Reminds them that their so-called pretty world is nothing but a pile of lies.

My stomach grumbles reminding me that it exists and is very upset with me. A glance at the clock tells me it's ten at night. The TV is silent. Either my dad crashed or he left. Either way, I can go eat and put some ice on my damn head.

All the lights are on downstairs, but even though I strain my ears, I can't hear any movement. Despite the silence, I still walk quietly, keeping my feet near the wall as I glide down the stairs. If my dad catches me out of my room, it'll be bad. I'm too old for grounding, but getting my ass beat again is not outside the realm of possibility.

I pad across the worn carpet into the kitchen without seeing my dad. My heart is pounding in my throat. A quick peek outside confirms that he's definitely still here. A few beers and an early morning wake up means he's out cold. Still I grab an ice pack from the freezer and let the soothing ice cool my head while I make myself a quick dinner. It's not much, but the sandwich will fill me up enough that I can sleep. I swipe a soda and a half-brown banana on the way out.

I disappear upstairs as quietly as I can, juggling my dinner all the way. I hear movement downstairs just as I slip into my bedroom. My hands are shaking so bad I barely keep from dropping my food. The lock makes a quiet rasping sound as I slide the bolt into place. I press my ear to the door and listen as my dad shuffles around downstairs for a bit before retreating once again to his bedroom. For a moment, I wonder if he heard me or just walking in his sleep. If he pees on the carpet again, I'm going to be so mad.

I barely taste the food as I cram it into my mouth. It's food. I'm hungry. My jacket is neatly draped over a chair, the devil's eye that spreads across the back glares at me. It's one of my favorite parts of the jacket. Red, black, flames, even stitched an upside-down pentagram around it. Upside down, of course, to piss off all the uppity super Christians. I even had one suggest an exorcism. Told me I was going to hell for my "sins". I flipped them the bird and told them I was already there. And to think they were offended.

An electronic pinging shatters the quiet and causes my heart to skip. With a shaking hand, I pick the phone up off my desk. Only a couple people have this number. Either something bad happened at Blake's, doubtful, or it's someone I don't want to talk to. I pull up the message and my heart freezes as the words burn across the screen.

Lela: I miss you.

CHAPTER FOUR

"What do you think, Mr. Monroe?"

Dammit. Mrs. Hampton only uses someone's last name if they've screwed up royally. I must have fallen asleep, again. I shouldn't be tired considering I've been home for the last few days. Thankfully suspension gave me a few days for the bruises to heal. Now, they are barely noticeable. At least I don't have to come up with another lie.

I stare at her dumbfounded while the other students laugh at my stupidity.

"Brit?" Mrs. Hampton turns to Brit. I'm not stalking my best friend's younger sister, but I do have a couple classes with her. Gives me an excuse to stare at her.

Her mom was a beauty queen and her dad was a state champion football player. I should know. I've seen the trophies and the pictures. Not that Brit's into the beauty scene, even though she has the looks and body for it. Like her brother, she's a pure athlete with brains. Curly black hair falls around her shoulders. Normally, she has it back, but today it brushes the tops of her shoulders. She claims it has a life of its own, but it fits her. Her skin is a shade lighter than her brothers and her eyes have a faint hazel tint. In a word, perfect. If Blake wouldn't kill me, and if I had the nerve, I'd tell her how I feel. Unfortunately, I'm not in the friend-zone. I'm in the "you're a brother to me" zone.

"Yes, Mrs. Hampton?"

"Would you please explain to Mr. Monroe what is so important about the Napoleonic Wars?" More laughter, more shame. I grind my teeth and think black thoughts.

"Certainly," Brit says happily. Everything she does is done with glee, and of course, perfectly. If I hadn't known her since we were little, I'd probably hate her for how perfect she is. She's even perfectly nice. To everyone. Seriously don't get it, but whatever.

Brit continues on about the Napoleonic wars oblivious to the fact that most of us don't care. I don't even bother listening. My grade is so far in the tank, listening to her isn't going to fix it. Besides, who gives a crap? Napoleon was a short loser who decided to attack a bunch of people and got his ass kicked. Seriously, who cares about the rest of that other garbage?

Mrs. Hampton glares at me over the rims of her glasses. I stifle a yawn. Brit gives me the stinkeye, I've never been able to get anything past her. I pretend to pay attention and end up doodling in my notebook.

I breathe a silent sigh of relief when she finally stops. I give her a lazy smile and she rolls her eyes at me. I know I should pay attention, get good grades and that stuff, but I frankly don't care. Good grades won't make me smarter, they're just a stupid badge that I can wave in people's faces to prove that I'm special or some crap like that. Reality is, nobody gives a damn if I got an A in some history class in high school. Sure, it might help me get into a college, but really, it doesn't do much else. Doesn't really prepare me for the real world full of monsters and Lela's. Besides, it's not like I'll need it. Not much need for history working in a garage. All they care about is does the engine run and if the body looks nice

Seriously, who gives a fuck about Napoleon?

I look up at the clock and bite off a quiet curse. All of this and I still have fifteen minutes before class ends. Jesus Christ, will it never end? I just want to get out of here. Mrs. Hampton gives up on keeping me focused and continues with the lesson. I tune it out.

Class ends after an eternity. It's touch and go there for a while, but I manage to survive. Students start packing up and heading toward the door. I try to make a stealthy exit, but Mrs. Hampton is waiting for me.

"Julius, I need to speak with you."

The announcement is met with the usual jeers and catcalls. I resist giving them the bird as I wait for the herd of students to leave. Once the classroom is empty, Mrs. Hampton fixes me with her hard stare. For being short, she still manages to scare the crap out of me. I force my feet to stop shuffling. They don't listen. Traitors.

"Now, Julius. You have a serious problem. The year has just started and you are already failing. Your previous teachers may have allowed you to squeak by, but not me."

I shrug noncommittally. I figure there's no point arguing. She's made up her mind.

"Now, if you need help, you can always stay after school and for tutoring. There are several groups you can join."

"I have a job," I say to my feet.

"Well, you have a choice. I realize that a lot of kids your age have jobs, but you need to seriously consider your grades too." She angles her head to try and catch my eye. I manage to keep ahead of her. I don't want to see the look of disapproval on her face. How can she understand that my job is the only thing I have? My dad can't keep a job to save his ass. If I don't bring in regular money, we end up on the street. Homework is the last thing on my mind.

"Ok, I get it. You don't want to talk about it. But seriously, Julius. If you want to graduate, you need to get your grade up. That means coming to class, turning in your homework, and answering when called on."

I keep my mouth shut and refuse to meet her gaze. She gets the hint and doesn't press anymore. She hands me a hall pass and I make my escape. Brit appears out of nowhere.

"Julius?"

I don't look at her. "What?" It comes out angrier than it should, but I'm mad.

"I heard you and Mrs. H talking. I would be happy to help you study. If you want to meet in the library after school today, I could…"

I interrupt her. "Can't." Great, now I've got another one breathing down my neck, bad enough that Mrs. H is jumping on me, now I have Brit doing it too.

Her steps falter and I smirk.

"Why not?" she asks.

I still don't look at her. I can feel her frustration mounting. "Got a job."

She rolls her eyes. "I know. Duh. Maybe I can talk to my dad and work something out?"

"If I don't work. I don't get paid. Your dad isn't going to pay me to study." I look down at her, my face twisted in a sneer, challenging. I shouldn't be mean to her, but I'm just so fed up with everything. Her feet stop and I keep walking. I should apologize, but I don't.

I leave her standing in the hallway and make my way to my next class. I might be failing history, but I'm getting a straight "A" in art. Hell, it's the only class that I feel like I fit in.

A quick glance shows Brit's retreating form. Good, she's out of my hair for now. I hurry off to class, my brain brimming with ideas for my next project. Something dark to go with my jacket. I'll have to make it subtle, so nobody gets too pissy with me. Last thing I need is for the morality police to come give me shit about something else.

Wait. Why do I care? It'll be art. They won't be able to touch it. A grin stretches across my face. The idea I have, if I do it right— big if—is gonna kick so much ass. Just like my jacket. If I ever finish it. But that's part of the whole thing. It changes, reflecting my life, my hell.

I look down at the word "Hate" embroidered on my sleeve in hues of red and black from elbow to wrist. The thorns encircling the letters were a pain, but I got it just right. The other sleeve has "No Love" in matching script and colors. The thorns curling around the letters and up both sleeves give me an idea for my art project. Of course, my favorite part is the upside-down pentagram with the devil's eye in the middle of my back. I look down at my watch. Damn. I'm going to be so late.

Painting a car should be easy, larger surface area, less need to be careful. Not quite. It's a delicate process and if you do it wrong, you have to start all over. I've only had to do that once. It's one of those lessons you never forget. Then there's pinstriping. Sure you can use a vinyl decal and get some nice looking lines, but when you have to do custom stuff, you have to do it free hand. Talk about delicate. Most of Mr. T's clients insist on a custom design, which is where I come in.

I read somewhere that in order to get a smooth line you should drink a beer first. Nothing super strong, just enough to steady the hand when you do the strokes. Having the right kind of paint is essential too. Mr. T doesn't let anyone drink on the job, so alcohol is not an option. At least I have several rags in case I mess up. The design won't be permanent until it is sealed anyway. Still, the fewer mistakes I make, the faster I'll get this done.

I'm leaning lightly across the hood painting. I could ask Mr. T to remove it, but I want to be able see how it'll look on the car. My back is screaming at me, so I know it's time to shift positions and stretch.

My back pops as I straighten. My eye follows the line I've painted. The striping starts at the trunk and goes the length of the Mustang and ends at the front of the car. Right now, I'm lining up the roof stripes with the hood. Strips of tape mark off my work area so I can keep the lines straight. I've got the shop radio loaded with my favorite band, Pain Splatter. The sound helps me focus. I could listen to anything, but there is something about screaming guitars that fits working on a classic car. Mouthing the lyrics to their newest song, I bend over the hood and get back to work.

I'm so absorbed in painting that I don't even notice that someone has entered the shop until Mr. T kills the music.

"Hey Brit! Didn't expect to see you here. Here to help your old man out?" My hand pauses mid-stroke and I quickly lift the brush from the hood.

"Not this time, I was looking for Julius."

Dammit! I am going to get so much hell for how I acted earlier.

"What did he do this time?" He asks. It's half a joke. He knows I suck at school. If he didn't need so much help, he'd probably insist I stay in class instead of skipping. It's one of the few things that he and Mrs. T ever argue about, at least while I'm around. Though considering the type of people they are, I doubt they argue about much. Except me, that is. The troublemaker.

"Oh, the usual," she replies. I can almost hear her roll her eyes. Her footsteps draw near and circle the car.

"Don't touch. Some of the paint is still drying," I say without looking up. Can never be too careful.

"Did you do all this?" Her voice is near my left side.

"Some. Mostly the pinstriping. It's delicate work and I need to concentrate." There, that should shut her up.

"How much longer will it take?" Great, she didn't shut up.

"As long as it takes," I say applying the brush carefully to the hood.

"Well, I was hoping we could do some studying," she says.

With a sigh I stand up straight and stretch. "You're not going to leave me alone are you?" I say with a glare.

She smiles and I swear there is a mischievous twinkle in her eyes. It ratchets her hotness level up a few notches more. I smash that thought out of my head. One of these days I'll stop mooning over her. Besides, even if she felt that way about me, I'm a mess and part of being with me is dealing with my dad.

"Fine. Guess I'm too distracted to finish anyway."

"Awesome, we can start once you're cleaned up," she says wrinkling her nose in a cute way.

She turns and picks her way toward the office, her skirt swaying with each step. I screw my eyes shut to block out the sight. Why did Blake's little, snot-nosed, annoying baby sister have to grow up to be so hot? It's like the universe hates me. Just thinking about it ruins my good mood from painting. With a grumbled curse, I pack up my brushes and paints and head into the bathroom to change.

When I emerge, Brit is sitting in the office chatting with Blake. You couldn't tell they were related. She's a good several inches shorter and slender where he is built like a truck. He definitely takes after his dad and will probably be sporting the same paunch as his dad in a few years. I've seen some of the pictures of their mom from when she was younger, and I can tell that Brit has her looks. Good thing too because Blake would make an ugly girl.

I wrap my knuckles on the window as I pass. Brit jumps at the sound and turns toward me with a glare. Blake rolls his eyes over her head and gives me a wink. He ruffles Brit's hair and she elbows him in the gut.

"Ok. Let's get this over with," I grumble as she walks out of the office. "We're kind of short of table space in here, but I'm sure we can rig up something."

Brit wrinkles her nose again. "Um. No. This place is too messy and you'll get distracted."

"Whatever," I say flatly. I won't get distracted, this is my home turf. I want to be somewhere I'm comfortable and not at a disadvantage.

Her glare deepens as we head toward the bay door. We pass Mr. T on the way out. He's finishing up the pinstriping and fixing my mistakes.

"Catch ya round, Mr. T." I wave as I pass.

"Later, Tiger." He glances at me as I pass.

Brit gives him a quick hug and we pass out into the sunlight. I squint as my eyes adjust.

"So where to? I don't have a car." Please don't say the library.

"The library of course," she states cheerily. I'm certain I hear a note of triumph in her voice. "We'll take my car."

The car is way too nice for a high schooler to be driving. It's a cherry red convertible. Of course, it looked like crap when it was hauled in here. I remember working on it with Mr. T. We decided to give it to Brit for her sweet sixteen birthday present. She was so excited she gave us all huge hugs. It was the first time I noticed how gorgeous she was. Just holding her set my brain on fire.

The weather is nice, the stifling heat of summer is gone, and Brit has the top down. She doesn't say a word as she slides into the driver's seat. I pause at the door and she looks up at me expectantly. With a sigh, I settle into the passenger seat. I'm sure I look ridiculous sitting next to her, but I can't help noticing the wind blowing her hair. I know I'm going to hate which ever guy she ends up with. I just know it. Granted, they'll have to be a great guy to get past Blake and Mr. T, so I'll have to hate them for that too. I know I'd never pass muster with those two. They like me. Hell, they're almost like family, but I know I'm not worth anything. She deserves someone better.

CHAPTER FIVE

The Wellsville Public Library is an underwhelming structure, as are most buildings in town. Designed in a quasi-old style that never looked right, more like a parking garage than anything else. The city doesn't have the money, or desire, to fix it, so they leave it the way it is. Besides, they needed a new football stadium for the high school. The Wellsville Warriors. Rah rah and all that crap.

Brit parks in the mostly empty parking lot. Nobody goes to the library much. She could have parked sideways and still left enough spaces for everyone else. But instead, she pulls neatly into the spot before killing the engine.

I turn my attention to the library. I haven't set foot in this place in a couple years. I'm not into online stuff and reading isn't my thing either. Most kids my age either go there to play online (away from their parents) or to make out in the stacks.

The smell of dust and old books fills my nose as we open the door. Brit leads me to a table in one of the rooms reserved for meetings. Her short brown ponytail bounces with each perky step as she carries a stack of textbooks to the table. I'm not carrying anything. I left mine at school.

I sit down and prop my feet on the table. Brit stares at me, eyes narrowed. I look at her and smirk. Her lips twitch and I know she wants to smile, but is too stubborn to give in. She knows I'm being a jerk.

"What?" I give her an innocent look.

"Will you please take this seriously?" She passes a book to me and sits down, smoothing her skirt. Her blouse is cut low enough that my eyes are drawn downward, and I have to force myself to focus.

I thump my feet to the ground. She jumps. I smile, feigning innocence.

"Why should I? Why should I take any of this seriously?" I refuse to make this easy on her. She practically stalked me to drag me out here. Besides, I just don't give a crap. She might, but to me, it's all meaningless bull they cram down our throats and then pat themselves on the back for a job well done. Not me.

"Don't you want to graduate?"

Maybe this will be my way out.

"As a matter of fact," I say as I lean toward her. "I don't care. I work in a fucking shop painting cars. I don't give a damn about Napoleon and all that other shit." I watch her wilt under my tirade. A part of me feels bad, but I'm really just tired of it all and she makes an easy target. I squash my guilt down.

"If you don't care, why did you come with me?" Her voice quavers a little and tears glisten in her eyes. She looks vulnerable and small. My anger starts to crumble and I want nothing more than to hold her and make it better. Stupid brain. She's not helpless. She's Brit. She's smart, tough, and beautiful. Me? I'm broken, weak, stupid . Not for the first time, I wonder if running off with Lela would have been better. I would have been away from my dad and away from Brit. Until he found us, I'd be free of him and I wouldn't hurt her.

"Fine." It's comes out as growl, my voice husky from the despair clawing at my insides. "Let's get this over with."

A small smile spreads across her lips like the sun after a rainstorm. I struggle to keep my face in its usual glare. It's hard. Her smile is infectious and I feel it trying to lift me up, like it always does. I look away before it can break the wall holding everything back. If I'm angry, I can't feel. If I can't feel, I'll survive. And most of all, I don't want her pity. That would be worse than anything. That she only loves me like a brother is bad enough, but those perfect eyes of hers filled with pity as I crumble before her is more than I can bear.

I can't breathe. I feel trapped. I have to get out of here. My chair crashes to the ground as I shove myself to my feet. My heart pounds in my chest and I fight against the rising panic. Brit looks at me, her eyes concerned.

"Julius?" Her voice is small in my ears. Her eyes are filled with concern and underneath that is fear. She's scared of me, of what I might do.

Anger swells inside of me. Brit has never been scared of me. Ever. I start pacing back and forth, my hand running through my hair. I want to squeeze my head until it all goes away. Brit is never scared of anything. This is the girl who jumped off the high dive when she could barely swim just because she could.

"Dammit!" I slam my hand into the table. Brit jumps.

"Julius?" she says again, her voice unsteady.

I gulp in air and try and slow my raging brain.

"What's wrong, Julius?" Her voice is a little steadier, but the fear is there and it twists in my gut.

"This is stupid," my voice trembles. It makes me sick. I'm so weak and stupid. "I'm sorry. I can't do this."

"Julius," Brit pleads. "Talk to me. What's going on?"

Why can't she see I'm a lost cause? This is such a dumb idea. I'm not good enough and she's wasting her time.

I slap the table in frustration. "This whole thing. It's stupid. It's a waste of fucking time. Frankly, school is the least of my worries right now and pretending to give a damn about it is stupid!" The last word lashes out of my mouth.

Brit slumps into her chair. She wipes a tear off her cheek with her palm, smearing her mascara. The smudge makes her look more human, more normal, less perfect. The knife twists in my gut and I feel sick to my stomach. I sit down with a sigh, the hard plastic back digs into my spine. I don't even care. I'm a jerk. Again. I slam a lid on the monster and force myself back to equilibrium. It's hard as hell, but I manage. I'm surprised my teeth don't crack with how hard I'm clenching my jaw.

I raise my eyes up to her, my glare firm. She's hunched over, submissive, her eyes down-turned. Her hope crushed beneath my hate. I feel ashamed. She's one of the few people who actually cares and I screwed it up by being a dick. I stand back up. Time to cut my losses and get the hell out of here. Her shoulders tense as if expecting a blow. It's a subtle movement and one I wouldn't have seen if I wasn't paying attention. Makes me wonder what happened to her. Who made her scared. Who her monster is. I know it's nobody in her house. I've known the Thompsons and they are a happy, loving family. So different from mine.

"I'm sorry." Her voice is quiet, weak, and thick with unshed tears.

There is so much in those two tiny words. I know her secret. It's the same one I have. Behind that perfect mask is a fear that knifes through me. I recognize it and it terrifies me. I have to leave before I make another mistake like Lela.

"Yeah," I manage. "Listen, I'll just walk home. You don't need to worry about me."

Brit doesn't say anything. She just sits there staring at her lap, occasionally wiping her nose with the back of her hand. I leave and head out into the cooling evening air. I should apologize. I don't.

It's a good two miles home, but not the longest I've had to walk. My dad left me by the side of the road one time. I was ten. He was drunk and got mad. Pulled over, wrenched the door open and threw me down into the ditch and then sped off. I walked five miles before someone saw me and gave me a ride. I can't even remember what I said.

I'm halfway home when my phone pings with a new text. My feet stumble as I read the screen.

Lela: I'm lonely.

My breath freezes in my lungs and I slump against a tree. My mind blanking as I'm overwhelmed by shame, dark and black. It oozes over my defenses. I choke back a sob and try to still my trembling hands as I force myself to clear the message. A small part of me wants to respond, but I don't. I can't. What she wants is not anything that I can give her. I can't fix her problem anymore. I don't think I ever could. I was comfort in the dark after the monster. Now, she's free and I'm not. She left. I stayed.

But a part of her still needs me. Those two words are enough to tell me that. I can't go through with this anymore. I know it's wrong. On some level, I'm sure she knows it's wrong. I couldn't protect her from my father, and I couldn't protect myself from her. The whole situation is so messed up.

I push myself up and stumble towards home. I hope my father isn't home. I can't deal with him or life at the moment. Not with Lela's text burning in my brain. And definitely not perfect Brit and her secret. I know I can't involved, but I know she's feeling alone. Vulnerable. Afraid.

I know she's probably left the library by now, but a part of me wants to go back. It's stupid. I'm stupid. Nothing good will come of me being a nice guy. Anytime I try, life bitch-slaps me back down. It's just not worth it. She's not worth it.

But then I remember the flinch. I know I was being a dick, but she flinched. Normal people don't flinch. Hell, she was standing up to me until I pushed it. Let the monster peak out just a bit and she shut down like I had hit her.

And that's when I know I'll get involved. I can't let someone like Brit end up like me, full of shame and hate. She doesn't deserve it. I can't believe I'm even thinking this. She is one of them. The upper elite who have it all and I'm a loser nobody. But as annoyingly perky as she is, I know it's a lie.

CHAPTER SIX

After Lela's text, I shouldn't be answering the phone at three in the morning, but my hand responds before my brain realizes what it's doing.

"Hello?" I mumble into the phone.

"Jules," my dad slurs. "You need to pick me up." His voice stumbles over the words, but I know his drunk speak.

"Where's the car, dad?" I groan into the phone.

Silence. I look at the phone and the call has disconnected. Great, my dad just hung up the phone and now I have to figure out which bar he was at. I stare at the phone a few minutes trying to get my brain to stop resembling a bucket of sludge and actually turn into something useful. Like a brain. Or a car.

Maybe I'll get lucky and he'll call back. I wait a few more minutes before I hit the call back button. I hope someone answers.

"Phillips speaking," A bored voice answers.

"Um," I stutter. "My dad just called me…"

"Is this Julius?"

"Yes, sir." Always best to answer politely when talking to the police.

"Yeah, sorry about that. Your dad's a bit out of it. Snoring actually. Why don't you go back to bed. If you need a ride we can send someone by to pick you up in the morning."

I pause. It would be so easy to give in and sleep. But I know my dad. He wants me to pick him up. It's times like these that I want to leave him there. Let him stew until they finally let him out and by the time he gets home, I'm gone. Not sure where I would go, maybe Blake's, maybe somewhere far away. Some place he can't find me. Which is harder than it sounds. I don't have any options with even less money to do it with.

"Thank you, but I think it would be best if I took him home."

Officer Phillips sighs quietly. "Ok. His car's at the bar where we picked him up. Give me a few minutes and I'll be by to pick you up."

Again. I don't say it aloud, but it's not the first time I've had a ride in the middle of the night to pick up my father.

I get dressed and sit down on the front steps and wait for the cruiser to pull up. The headlights splashing across my eyelids jolt me awake. My jaw pops when I yawn and stretch, working out the kink out of my neck. I slide into the passenger seat and Phillips hands me a steaming cup of coffee. It's a small gesture of kindness, but I'm grateful nonetheless.

"Thanks," I say, warming my hands on the styrofoam.

Phillips smiles, his face lit from the instrument panel. It distorts his features so he looks almost alien. Either that or I'm hallucinating from lack of sleep. I avert my eyes and focus on my coffee.

"Sure thing," he says. "Figured you could use it."

I nod and let the burning liquid chase away the chill.

"Listen," Phillips starts as we head off toward my dad's car. "I want to talk to you about your dad."

"Yeah? What about him?" I have a feeling I know what he's going to say. It's not like it hasn't been said a thousand times to me over the years.

"I'm sure other people have talked to you about this before."

Here it comes.

"Your dad needs help, son. I know I'm the new guy on the force, but even I know what he's doing is wrong."

Maybe it's the son comment, maybe it's his tone of voice, maybe it's just lack of sleep. Whatever it is, I am not going to sit here and listen to this cop.

"Listen," I snap. "I appreciate the coffee and the ride, but it's none of your business. It's not like this happens all the time. Everyone has a bad day once in a while." My mouth is babbling and I shut it before I tell him what else my dad has done. At least the bruises are gone this time.

Phillips takes a couple deep breathes and continues driving. I glance over and his mouth in a tight line, hands gripping the wheel. Julius: One. Cops: Zero. This time. Looking at him more closely, I realize how big he is. His uniform strains against the muscles as they bunch with tension. I should apologize before he crushes me. It's not his fault. He doesn't know what my dad has been through. I know I try to avoid him as much as possible, but at the end of it all, I always come back. He knows that. And when I don't, he finds me and drags me home. It isn't the greatest situation, I mean seriously, I'm getting a ride with a cop to pick up my dad's car that got left at a bar when he was arrested. Probably for drunk and disorderly, his usual.

God, my life is so messed up. At least the cop gave me some coffee.

"I'm…" I take a drink. "I'm sorry. I shouldn't have jumped on ya like that. It's just. I don't know."

Phillips glances at me. "It's ok, kid. I understand."

Ok, now I'm feeling awkward. Good one, Julius. Luckily, I'm saved from anymore embarrassment as we pull up to dad's rusty car. If he didn't hate them so much, and we had the money, I'd have my dad take it to Mr. T's shop. Might keep it from snowing inside the car during the winter.

Phillips puts his hand on my arm as I start to get out of the cruiser.

"If you need to talk," he says, handing me a business card. "Call. Ok?"

I take the card and slip it into my jacket pocket without looking.

"Sure thing," I say stepping out into the chilly night air. "Oh, and thanks for the coffee."

I close the door before he can respond and shuffle over to my dad's car. The inside of the car smells like beer and mold. Nice. I pump the gas a couple times and crank the engine. It sputters, almost dies. Phillips's cruiser idles next to me. He's waiting to make sure the car starts. Nice guy. I rev the engine to keep it running and Phillips finally pulls away leaving me in the parking lot.

I kick on the heater, but I know it's a futile gesture. The stupid thing doesn't work for crap anyway. Busted heater coil or something, I don't know. Mr. T explained it to me when I asked about it, most of it didn't make sense.

True to form, the heater starts its pathetic attempt at warming the interior of the car by the time I reach the police station. Figures. Which means, by the time I get my dad, the car will be cold again. So need to get that stupid thing fixed.

The car wheezes and coughs after I kill the engine. The way it sounds, it's a small miracle it's even still functional. One of these days it's going to stop working completely. Then my dad will get pissed and probably blame it on me.

Not that I drive the car except to pick him up from the police station or the bar. Otherwise he's using it and I'm walking or hitching a ride. One of these days I'll have enough to get something of my own. At the rate I'm saving, I should have enough by the time I'm thirty-five.

After tonight, sorry this morning, it'll be thirty-six. Jesus, I hate this crap. I mutter a stream of curses as I haul my tired butt up the stairs. At least they know I'm coming. Wonder if they'll give me a discount? Bail your drunken father out of jail five times and the sixth one free. I chuckle to myself as I'm buzzed in.

It's six by the time I get all the paperwork filled out, my bank account diminished, and my dad awake and ready to go. I should just skip school and sleep. My eyes are gritty and heavy. Unless I get a caffeine infusion, I doubt I'll survive.

"Give me the keys," my dad grumbles as we reach the car.

"Dad," I say for the umpteenth time. "They said that you shouldn't drive. I don't want to get in trouble"

My dad pushes up against me, his breath foul, his bloodshot eyes narrowed in anger.

"I don't give a goddamn what they said. You'll give me the keys, or I'll beat your ass with a ball bat. Understand?"

I nod, swallowing the giant lump forming in my throat, and hand them over. He stumbles slightly as he walks the last few feet to the car, the keys dangling loosely in his hand. His knuckles are scraped from whatever altercation he got into to land him in jail this time. The car rocks slightly as we get in. My father sits there for a moment and I think he's fallen asleep. The smell of stale sweat and the foul reek of the alcohol on his breath climbs up my nose, making my eyes water. If I didn't think he'd kill me, I would so hose him down. God, he stinks.

"I'm hungry," he slurs.

"Well, I could drive us home and…"

"No," he growls. "I'll drive."

I make sure my seatbelt is secure before he lurches the car out the parking lot. God, I hope we don't die. The headlights swerve back and forth as we head off in search of food. Dammit, I'm going to be late to school again.

CHAPTER SEVEN

Wellsville High isn't a big school by any means. My graduating class is about one hundred fifty kids all told. Might end up being one hundred forty-nine if I don't pull my grades out the gutter. Despite its relative small size, the hallways are still crowded between classes. The tile floors and metal lockers amplifying the voices of the students into an almost deafening roar. Years of practice allows me to move easily through the congested hallways, the only hindrance being underclassmen. Freshmen are still confused by the change of scenery and have a tendency to stand idly by as you try to navigate the press of bodies. A few well-placed elbows and they get the hint and start moving like the drones they are.

As a senior, I am able to nimbly slip between slower moving students on my way to my next class. That and my jacket discourages anyone from walking too close. Thankfully, it's Algebra and I don't have to worry about Miss Perfect ruining my day.

A large hand grabs me by the shoulder and yanks me off course and into a side hallway.

My breath slams out of my lungs as my back crashes into a locker. The bang of the rattling door is swallowed up by the ambient roar of the crowded main hallway. Nobody notices or if they do, they keep their eyes forward and don't say anything. An arm presses under my chin, forcing my head up and to the side. I fight the rising panic as my throat is constricted. An image of my father's hands closing around my neck flashes through my mind. For a moment, I think it's him.

"Hey, Greg, hurry up man. I can't be late or coach'll chew my ass again." A voice says off to my left, shattering illusion.

The arm belongs to Greg, which means I'm in some serious trouble. I can't make out who else is with him, but I have a good idea. I don't know what they want with me, but with him it could be anything. In this case, it's probably my jacket. Knowing him, he was probably one of the people behind that whole fiasco with Dr. Stevens.

Greg's a jerk on and off the field. If his dad wasn't president of the school board, he would have been kicked off the football team a long time ago. "Shut up, Lewis. This ain't gonna take long." Greg removes his arm and I slump to the floor, gasping.

"What's the matter, Greg? Run out of freshmen to molest?"

Me and my stupid mouth. My idiocy is rewarded by Greg grabbing my hair and wrenching my head back.

"Listen, freak!" he hisses, inches from my face. "You stay the hell away from my girlfriend, you hear me?"

"No problem," I fire back. "I didn't even know you liked girls."

Greg growls in anger and raises his fist to knock me into next week. With as big as he is, I'll be lucky if he doesn't kill me. Lewis grabs his arm before he can deliver the death blow.

"Greg. Man," he whispers. "Be careful. If coach finds out you're fightin' again, he's likely to suspend you!"

Greg continues to strain against his friend before relaxing his hand and releasing my hair. He shoves me as he stands up and I slam into the locker again. Somehow he manages to calm himself from his testosterone fueled rage. I guess it will add a couple more personal fouls to his growing total come game day.

"Don't screw with me, punk!" Greg snaps, looming over me, his fists clenched at his side. "Brit's mine."

"What?" The words catch in my throat as the reality dawns on me. Brit is dating Greg.

He must see the thoughts exploding across my face as my heart implodes because a large, savage grin splits his face. He's won and he knows it.

"What?" He gloats. "You thought you had a chance with her? You weren't good enough for your crack-headed mom. Only reason she even talks to you is because you work for her dad."

I surge up to my feet, rage flowing through my veins, only to get shoved back to the ground like I'm nothing. Greg doesn't even break a sweat. I force myself to still even as he stares down at me with a challenging stare.

The warning bell reverberates down the hall. As one, Greg and his cronies glance up.

"Come on, man," Lewis pleads as he tugs on Greg's arm. "We gotta get to class!"

"Yeah, let's leave this trash for the custodians to pick up," one of his sycophants, Drake I think, pipes up.

Greg chuckles and fist-bumps his buddies. "Good one, man. Yeah, he's nothing." He smirks over his shoulder at me.

Yup, that's me. Nothing. Trash. I smash down the rage threatening to burst over me. The last thing I need is to do something really stupid. I imagine different scenarios where I kick his ass and humiliate him as he and his buddies head toward class. Occasionally one will turn to see if I'm still there. I am. They laugh and turn a corner. One of these days.

With a grunt, I push myself off the floor and retrieve my fallen books. I head toward my next class. I glance at the textbooks in my hand. My social studies textbook glares at me with its evil blue and orange cover. I quietly snarl back as I trudge down the hall and take a detour toward the bathroom. The adrenaline is dumping from my system and I need to clear my head before walking into class.

I manage to stumble into the bathroom, the stench slithers up my nose. God, I hate the bathrooms here. I've seen some disgusting stuff in my life, but nothing compares to a high school boys bathroom. People should get a medal of honor just walking in the door.

I careen over to the sink and lean my hands against it. I grip the sides so hard, my knuckles turn white. The shaking hits me so hard I almost collapse. I lean my forehead against the cool mirror as rage filled thoughts pour through my brain. It takes all I have to keep from smashing my hand through the mirror.

Hot tears squeeze out of my eyes and fall to the sink. Shame. Fear. Hate. All mixed together in a putrid slurry in my brain. I force it all down. Force myself back to center. I hit the faucet and scrub the tear-stains from my eyes. Last thing I need is to have people think I'm a whimp.

Social studies was boring, as usual. The only difference was Brit trying to catch my eye. Felt my phone vibrate a couple times, but after getting the text from Lela, I'm not too keen on looking at it during school hours. Her messages, which have been hitting my phone every couple days, fill me with a mixture of regret and shame. I don't crack during school.

Greg stalks me for part of the day, but I manage to lose him and his cronies. Seriously, those guys need a life but I'm not tough enough to stand toe to toe with them and have a chance of surviving. I figure if I ignore them long enough, and avoid Brit, they won't be able to do anything.

The walk to the shop is cold and long. I'm going to need to figure out transportation before it gets too cold. Hate to bother Blake, but he's the only person I know that would give me a ride. Getting a ride with Brit would increase the potential of Greg using my face for a punching bag so that option is eliminated on principle.

I push thoughts of Brit from my head as I draw near the garage. There's a sleek, purple sports car in the lot. It doesn't have any damage, so I can only assume it's a visitor and not a customer. I really should know more about cars, but I'm more interested in painting them than anything else.

Mr. T has a mini-van in the shop. Looks like some soccer mom got t-boned. Nice dent on the passenger side. Doesn't look like it'll take much more than a new door and then some sanding and paint matching. If the parts are available, it should only take a couple days max.

I head towards the back of the shop to get changed. Blake's in the office as usual. What's unusual is the man leaning casually on the desk talking to him. Haven't seen him around, but it's obvious that they know each other. The guy's big. Maybe even bigger than Blake. Broad, muscular and dark skinned, an African-American Adonis. His white t-shirt strains to contain the muscles underneath. There's something familiar about the profile, but staring at the back of his bald head isn't giving me any clues. Blake's eyes flicker over to me and the man smoothly shifts away from the desk. It's a fluid almost like a dancer's movements. I lightly rap my knuckles on the window and Blake waves me in.

"Hey Blake! Is your dad around?" Blake's friend turns to face me as I step into the now crowded office and I almost choke when I recognize him. It's Phillips. The guy gave me a ride a couple days ago. I hope he doesn't recognize me.

"Nope. Went on a parts run." Blake's face colors a little as he looks at his friend. "Oh, Julius. This is Marcus."

Marcus smiles at me and lifts a large paw to shake my hand. If he wanted, he could crush my fingers without even trying. Despite his size, his grip is firm but gentle.

"It's a pleasure to meet you," he says, his voice is smooth and deep. "Blake has told me a lot about you."

I smile when I realize he's not going to rat me out. "Don't believe anything he tells you. It's all bullshit."

Marcus' laugh fills the tiny room. "He did warn me that you were a pain in the ass."

Blake's eyes widen in mock disbelief. "I never said that!" Marcus laughs even harder.

"You comin' to the gym later?" Marcus asks after his laughter subsides.

"Sure!" Blake responds with enthusiasm. I would never be that excited about exercise. There is something seriously wrong with him.

"Awesome. See you there!" Marcus turns back to me. "Nice meetin' ya, man. See ya around sometime." Blake watches him leave before turning back to me.

I slump into a chair with a sigh.

"Rough day?" He asks, rising from his chair to stretch.

"Eh. Some d-bag thought I was trying to steal his girlfriend. You know, the usual."

Blake laughs at me. I flip him the bird as he eases into the chair next to me, bumping my shoulder.

"You're serious?"

I give him a patient look. "Yeah, I'm serious. It was stupid too. He and two of his buddies tried to molest me in the hall."

Blake groans. "Oh god. Three d-bags? Let me guess, Greg, Lewis, and Drake?"

My scowl answers his question. I don't tell him that Brit's dating Greg. I figure it's her place to tell him if she wants. Of course, maybe it isn't that serious. Maybe Greg was lying.

"Oh man," Blake interrupts my thoughts. "Greg was such a punk his Freshman year. Thought he was all hot stuff. He had a lot of raw talent, but a nasty temper. We made him carry all our pads between practice for being a cocky little shit."

"Well, he hasn't changed," I grumble. "If anything, he's gotten worse."

Blake shakes his head. "That doesn't surprise me. Wish I could help you, man." Blake claps me on the shoulder before heaving himself out of the chair.

"God, you sound like an old man," I tease.

Blake chuckles and stretches tall, his fingers brushing the ceiling, before folding himself behind the desk.

"I could so outrun you," he says with a cocky grin.

"Provided you didn't break your hip," I fire back.

The tension that's been riding in my shoulders for days loosens as we toss silly insults back and forth. It helps banish Brit and Greg from my mind, even if it's only temporary, I take whatever respite I can get.

"Hey, Blake?" I say breaking the silence. I'm not sure I want to ask him, but I don't want to spend the weekend at my house. Not with my dad out of a job again.

Blake grunts.

"Can I crash at your place over the weekend?"

"Sure," Blake says. He saves me the embarrassment of having to make something up by not asking why.

"Thanks," I say.

Before too long, Mr. T shows up and drags me into the work bay to help with the soccer-mom mobile. I'd rather sit and hang with Blake all afternoon, but I need the money and Mr. T needs the help.

CHAPTER EIGHT

Blake's house is always warm and inviting; no matter when I show up or what shape I'm in when I arrive. The neighborhood isn't the fanciest, but all the houses have paint that isn't faded and peeling and lawns that are actual lawns and not dried dirt and weeds.

The Thompson house is well cared for. When Mr. T isn't working at the shop, he's fixing the place up while Mrs. T makes sure everything looks Martha Stewart perfect. The carpets, though worn, are always vacuumed. The shelves are always dusted and everything placed just so. It's actually a little creepy if you think about it too long.

"Thanks, man," I say as we walk to his front door, my backpack full of clothes.

Blake gives me grin and a playful head-slap. "I warned you I'd do that if you didn't stop saying that."

I respond with an elbow to the stomach which bounces harmlessly off the rocks he has for abs. I glare and flip him the bird just as Mrs. Thompson opens the door.

"Julius Franklin Monroe, we will not be having such inappropriate gestures in my house." Her glare is softened by the slight upturning of her lips.

"Sorry Mrs. T," I say with giant puppy dog eyes. "It'll never happen again, I swear." I make a small X over my heart before clasping my hands in front of me like a good little hooligan.

Mrs. T rolls her eyes but she's smiling when she turns away. "I'd tell you to help yourself to the fridge, but I figure you already knew that. You can thank Brit for setting up your bed."

Grabbing a biscuit from the fridge, I head for my home away from home, the Thompson's basement family room.

"I'll bring down some towels. Don't make a mess in there," Blake says, flashing me a grin before heading upstairs. "I don't want to clean up after you again. That damn hair clogs up the drain bad."

I almost flip him the bird but catch Mrs. T eyeballing so I turn it into an awkward hand flap as I disappear downstairs. Mrs T's girlish laughter follows me all the way to the bathroom. I needed this as a genuine smile pulls at my face. No matter my mood, just being here makes it all better. I wish I could bottle this up and save it for when my dad goes on his next rampage.

The shower helps wash all the dirt I gathered at the shop today. Although, I'm sure I'll spend the rest of my life with permanent stains from the grease and paint. There are worse things, I know, but there's something about being at Blake's that makes me want to clean up extra. Like, I don't want to smudge their perfect life.

I slip into an old pair of sweatpants that I brought with me. It's the closest to PJs as I get. I don't bother with a shirt. Stretching out on the futon, I lean my back against the wall and flip on the TV. My brain is still too frazzled to sleep. I flip channels trying to find something to keep my attention for longer than half a second.

Soft footsteps on the stairs signal the arrival of Brit.

"Hey," Brit says peaking around the corner. She stands there, arms crossed over her stomach. She's uncertain and I don't blame her. The last time we spoke I yelled at her.

"Hey, squirt," I respond, hoping to break the tension. She hates the nickname, and hell she's almost as tall as me now, but I don't know how else to tell her we're OK. Her eyes narrow a little and her nostrils flare at my comment. It's more cute than intimidating, but I know better. She'd kick my ass in a heartbeat.

Instead of punching me, she plops down next to me on the futon. Her hair is down and she's wearing sweats and a Hello

Kitty tank top. It's a cute look on her, not that I notice those things. Blake would kill me for checking out his sister. Still, it's hard not to notice her proximity when I can feel the heat from her arm centimeters from mine.

"So...um...we good?"

Brit's shoulders shift up in a half-hearted shrug. I don't see her move until she punches me square in the arm. It isn't a light punch either. Rage boils up and it's a fight to keep it in check. As it is, I still end up having to tighten a fist so hard my nails gouge my palm. I deserve it though. The pain. The humiliation. I crush those thoughts too. This is my happy place. Bad things don't happen here.

"You're still a big jerk," she says as she snuggles up next to me and puts her head on my shoulder. Her hair tickles my bare chest and I can smell the mint of her toothpaste. Her shampoo smells of spring flowers. Her tears dampen my shoulder.

"Are you ok?" I'm a little worried, she's normally more talkative and I haven't seen her cry in years. I keep flipping channels. It's more background noise than anything at this point.

She shakes her head no before grabbing the remote and killing the TV.

"Five hundred channels and not a damn thing to watch," I say when she tosses the remote next to us.

Brit snorts and wraps her arms around my waist and hugs me tight.

"You know, if you get snot on my shoulder, I'm totally going to make fun of you," I tease. I can't help it. Brit's weirding me out and I don't know how to deal with it. I want to make everything better, but I know I can't.

"Shut up, you jerk." She wipes her nose on my shoulder.

"Oh, that is so disgusting!" I grab the towel I was using to dry my hair and shove it in her face as I wipe the snot off my shoulder. Brit wipes her nose on my shoulder again and I pinch her ribs. She jumps with a shriek and slaps my chest. I poke her in the ribs again and she tackles me to the floor.

It ends fast. She's stronger and before I know it, I'm pinned on the floor with her on top of me. Her eyes are red rimmed, but she's smiling. I hear heavy footsteps on the stairs. Someone has decided to investigate.

"You'd be a lot cuter if you didn't have a big blob of snot hanging from your nose," I say with a grin.

Brit's eyes grow wide and she gets her hand up to her face just before she starts laughing and snorting. Pretty soon I'm laughing with her. She gets a wicked gleam in her eye just before she wipes her hands on my chest. This starts another one-sided wrestling match.

"You guys are weird, you know that?" Blake's voice freezes us in mid-wrestle before Brit collapses on me in an uncontrollable fit of laughter. She's laughing, crying, and blowing snot all over me and I'm laughing harder than I have in a long time. I wipe a tear from my eye and see Blake leaning against the wall with a big grin on his face.

"She started it!" I point dramatically to Brit which causes her to giggle.

Brit hiccups and laughs some more which sets me off in my own fit. Brit's laughing so hard, she slides off of me and onto the floor. One leg and arm still draped over me as she giggles and gasps into my shoulder. Blake's lips quirk.

"Mom says you need to get to bed." he says.

Brit sighs as she gets off of me and sits up. She's grinning at me like a lunatic and I grin back. Guess we both needed that. I pat her arm as I sit up.

"Go on, Squirt, or your mom'll get mad," I tell her with a smile.

Brit surprises me by giving me a big hug before racing upstairs.

"What was that all about?" Blake asks as I pull myself off the floor.

"Just blowing off some steam," I reply as I grab the towel and head back into the bathroom to wipe the snot off my chest.

Blake laughs from the other room. "Yeah, she mentioned being mad at you."

"Yeah," I reply as I look at the small crescent shaped scar on my collar bone, another memento of the Monster. My father was really upset when he saw what the Monster had done. I was eight. He threw a pair of scissors at me.

When the Monster went away, my father rushed me to the ER. He told the doctor that he had fallen asleep and that I was running with the scissors. The doctor gave me a lecture about being more careful as he stitched me up. I didn't tell him it was the Monster and that my father had thrown the scissors at me. I knew, even then, that nobody would believe me.

I sigh quietly as the memory sours the moment with Brit. I try to recall the moment, but the memory of the Monster and scissors overshadows any happiness that I was feeling. One of these days I'll understand why the he exists and what I did that put him in my life. I shake my head as I exit the bathroom.

"What's wrong man?" Blake says from the futon, his back propped against the wall. His gaze follows me as I walk into the room.

"Nothing. Just thinking," I say as settle in next to him. "By the way, your parents need to invest in some more channels. The selection sucks."

Blake snorts. "Yeah, I'll let 'em know." He nudges me with his shoulder. "Maybe if you didn't listen to such crappy music, your taste in movies would be better."

"What? Pain Splatter is an awesome band! Their music rocks!" I can't believe he just trashed my favorite band. Ok, yes I can believe it. I know he's messing with me. I go with it.

Blake snorts. "Music? That wall of noise? I've heard cats yowling that sounds better."

I laugh. "I'd kick your ass for that, but I wouldn't want to hurt your pretty boy looks. Girls might get depressed."

Blake rolls his eyes. "Yeah. Whatever, man. You couldn't even beat my sister."

"She cheated!" I counter with mock indignation.

"She still beat you," he says with a sly grin.

"Yeah, but she's your sister! You'd kick my ass!" No, he wouldn't but it's a good excuse for my poor performance.

"Never stopped you before." His comment freezes me in place.

He's right. Brit's strong, but I do outweigh her. I could have pinned her, but I didn't. Part of me didn't want to. The thought makes me even more uncomfortable.

"Yeah, well." I clear my throat. "She was wiping snot on me. Hard to fight someone when you've got nose-slime all over you."

And just like that, the tension breaks and everything is back to normal. Blake chuckles and flips on the TV.

"Yeah, she does cheat like that," he says with a smile. He flips a few channels. "You're right, this selection does blow."

"See?" I raise my arms dramatically.

Eventually we settle on a zombie flick. Can never go wrong with a good zombie movie. The gore and the screaming scantily clad babes distract us enough. Eventually, Blake can't take the horrible dialog and crappy special effects and leaves me to it. He grumbles about having to get up in the morning. I spread out on the futon and turn off the TV. The last thought I have before tumbling into sleep is of Brit. I smile into the dark until I start thinking about what Brit looks like, how her tank top hugged her body. The warmth of her lying on top of me. I try to run from those thoughts, but they follow me into sleep.

CHAPTER NINE

"Come on! It'll be fun!" I plead as we drive home from work.

"I am not driving you forty minutes to some dingy little bar so you can watch guys scream into microphones for an hour," Blake responds, impervious to my attempts to sway him.

"Well, duh! That's the point! Pain Splatter is that kind of band!"

Blake sighs. "Listen, I have plans. Marcus and I are supposed to hang out."

I try a different tactic. "Bring him along. Or better yet, just drop me off. I'll hitch a ride."

Blake shakes his head as we pull into his driveway. "No. First of all, Marcus and I have reservations. Second, I'm not leaving you to get a ride just to have it fall through at the last minute."

We get out of the car and head into the house.

"Come on. That was just one time and I paid for the gas."

"Not the point," Blake responds as we hang our coats by the door. "It was two in the morning."

Blake's right. It did suck, but I really want to go. I need to get out of the house. As much as I love staying here, I'm getting cabin fever. That and I love Pain Splatter.

Staying the weekend turned into a week. It happens like that sometimes, but living in the basement means I'm close to the washing machine. I've learned to check with everyone before I use it though. Don't want a repeat of finding Brit's underwear and bras in the dryer. The mental picture of her wearing said clothing is distracting and a little weird. She's always been Blake's little sister. I'm doing my best to think of her like that, but being around her so much lately is making it difficult.

"What are you guys arguing about?" She asks as she follows us into the living room.

I sit with a sigh on their overstuffed couch.

"Blake is being a pansy and doesn't want to drive me to a Pain Splatter concert. Something about him and Marcus having a date," I say with air quotes around the word date.

Brit and Blake share a look.

"What?" I ask sensing an unspoken dialog.

"Nothing. I gotta get cleaned up before I go meet Marcus for dinner."

Blake heads upstairs and Brit plops down next to me and rests her head on my shoulder. She's dressed in jeans and dark blue turtleneck. It's Friday and I'm surprised she's not getting ready to hang out with her friends.

"Didn't you have plans tonight?" I ask as I shift to give her a more comfortable point on my shoulder.

"Boys are dumb," Brit pouts.

Uh oh. "What happened?"

Brit launches into a diatribe about boys, friends, and canceled plans.

"Well, any guy who would stand you up is a moron," I say once she winds down.

Brit snorts. "Whatever."

"Seriously," I say as I rest my cheek on her head. "You're beautiful, smart, and funny. Any guy would be lucky to be with you."

"You're just saying that because you want a ride to the concert," Brit says shifting away from me and fixing me with a mock glare, arms crossed.

I give her a shocked expression. "Me? No, I would never be that subtle," I say with a smirk and a wink.

"Oh, so you don't want to go with me?" Brit says, arching her eyebrow at me expectantly.

My cheeks heat and I look away to hide the flurry of emotions. When I look at her my smirk is back.

"You drive, I'll buy," I say and give her another wink.

I'm rewarded with a slight coloring of her cheeks and it's her turn to look away for a moment. Brit bounces up.

"Well, if we're going on a date, I better get changed," She says as she dashes up the stairs.

"Wait!" I call after her, but she's already disappeared around the corner. Great. What the hell am I getting myself into? I trudge downstairs and change into something that doesn't smell like paint and motor oil.

Bit takes her time getting ready. I'm standing at the bottom of the stairs like an anxious date on prom night. My stomach is alive with butterflies. It's weird and disturbing. It's not like it's a real date. Hell, I'm not dressed up. For the hundredth time since Brit disappeared into her room, I wonder if she's just messing with me.

Brit turns the corner and my breath catches in my throat. She's dressed in a short skirt with leggings that show off the muscles in her calves. Under her jacket, she's wearing a form fitting top that accentuates her athletic figure. A black choker circles her neck with a sparkling gemstone in the center. The whole outfit is all blues and blacks. Dark eye shadow circles her eyes making the faint hazel in her eyes stand out stand out. Bright red lipstick draws my eyes to her mouth.

I've never seen her dressed like this and it's stunning. Her step falters when she sees me staring.

"I'm sorry," she stammers, suddenly uncertain. "I'll go change."

I shake myself out of my stupor and give her a smile.

"No," I say shaking my head. "It's perfect." As soon as the words leave my mouth, my cheeks heat and it's my turn to look away. I slam the lid shut on the weird feelings. This is Brit. Blake's sister. Definitely hands off, but damn is she gorgeous.

"Great!" Brit says happily and bounds down the stairs.

I breathe a silent sigh of relief as the world returns to normal. We're going out to have fun and get away from everything. It's not like it's a real date or anything. Brit walks into the kitchen and I catch myself watching the sway of her hips before mentally slapping myself. This is going to be a difficult night, but I'm not going to make Brit change. She wanted to go out, so we're going out. It's what friends do. Right?

I follow Brit into the kitchen were her mom is working on dinner. Mrs. T stares at us, a weird look on her face, while Brit spells out why she wants the car, where we're going, and when we'll be home. I see wheels turning in Mrs. T's head and for the first time I'm glad that Brit's dad isn't home. With the way Brit's dressed, I doubt he would let her out of the house.

"Please, Mom?" Brit lays on the charm and draws out the please.

Mrs. T has her arms crossed as she leans against the counter. Her body language saying she is not too keen on the idea of her only daughter driving out to a rock concert with a boy of dubious parenting such as myself. I keep my distance from Brit as we stand in the kitchen. I don't want to give her mom any ideas about my intentions.

"I promise it'll be ok," I say in an attempt to derail the thoughts that must be going through her mom's head. "We're just going to hang out for a bit and then we'll be home."

Mrs. T sighs. "Fine. Just be careful and I expect you home before midnight."

She gives her mom a dazzling smile and gives her a big hug. "Thank you, Mom."

Brit takes a set of keys from hook by the back door and heads into the garage. Mrs. T fixes me with a warning stare and I raise my hands slightly in supplication. A promise to be a gentleman and bring her only daughter home safe and with her virtue intact. In that moment, I'm more worried about what Mrs. T would do to me if anything happened to Brit than what Mr. T or Blake would do.

I duck into the garage as I hear Blake's tread on the stairs. I send up a silent prayer thanking the universe that Blake didn't see his sister dressed up. I know he wouldn't have let us out the house no matter what his mom said.

I plop down into the passenger seat and Brit looks at me, her features shadowed in the darkened car.

"Thank you."

I grin and pat her lightly on the knee. "Of course."

Brit snags my hand as I pull it back and gives it a tight squeeze. Her fingers are warm and soft before she lets go and backs the car onto the street.

CHAPTER TEN

"I can't believe you're taking me here for dinner?" Brit says in mock disdain as we sit in the molded plastic seats designed for people with significantly different bone structure than us, our tray of burgers and fries between us.

I stick my tongue out and Brit chucks a fry at me, laughing. We get a lot of stares from the other patrons. We look like a couple of dark stains in the overly-bright and plastic-coated burger joint. With my jacket sporting hate and her goth attire, I'm sure we look like a couple of Satan worshipers. The other patron's give us a wide berth.

A kid, no more than four, wanders up to us and stares. Brit gives him a dazzling smile and he shyly smiles back before running off to the safety of his mom who talks quietly to him and distracts his attention with a cheap plastic toy.

Brit watches him, a smile still on her face. "He's such a cute kid."

I glance over to the kid who's smashing the toy against the table with exuberance.

"Yeah, the mom's probably worried we'll turn her kid to the dark side." I wiggle my fingers at Brit like I'm casting a spell on her.

Brit chucks another fry at me and giggles.

"We do have cookies," Brit says pointing to the bag in the middle of the tray.

I put my face in my hands and groan. "I can't believe you just said that," I say with a laugh.

The rest of our meal is pretty uneventful, except for the occasional flying fry. It's easy to be with Brit. I don't have to fake it. I can be me and she doesn't care. Doesn't think I'm some pussy. Not for the first time, I catch myself looking at her. Really looking at her. She's beautiful, but untouchable and to be honest, I've got too much shit in my life to drag her down. She's too happy.

"What's wrong?" Brit asks breaking me out of my circling thoughts.

I shake my head. "Nothing. Don't worry about it. Just thoughts."

Brit hesitantly reaches for my hands. "Are you sure? If something is bothering you..."

"It's nothing," I say interrupting her. I disentangle my hands from hers. "Besides, you keep getting all mushy with me and people will start to talk."

Brit's eyes widen at my smirk and she looks away. "When does the concert start?"

I check the clock on my phone. "Another hour or so. Anywhere else you want to go?"

Anywhere else ends up being a miniature golf course in a mall, complete with goofy themes and rampaging children. Once again we stick out, but we have fun despite the whispers and stares. Brit catches me staring at her, for the hundredth time, and like every time before, she lets out a shy smile before looking away. A part of me wishes this could be every day. Just me and Brit having a good time, not a care in the world. But I know it can never happen.

After exhausting ourselves and hitting way over par, we leave the brightly lit mall and head out into the night.

Just as we're getting to the car, my phone buzzes. I delete Lela's message without reading it. I won't let her ruin this moment.

Brit maneuvers us into a spot in the packed parking lot. The ramshackle bar is less than impressive, but it's what is on the inside that counts. The bar used to be a big deal back in its heyday. Now the lights flicker on the big sign out front, the letters JD barely visible from the parking lot. Someone told me once that it used to boast these huge statues in the shape of those chrome women silhouettes you see on the back of semis.

Even back then it was a white trash kind of place.

Now, it's just an old bar, in an old part of town. All the businesses having moved to the power district full of glitter and d-bags. Frankly, I prefer this rat-infested dump over anything over there.

Brit scans the front of the building with obvious concern.

"It's not going to fall down is it?"

I laugh as I get out of the car. "Hasn't yet. You coming?"

Brit hesitates a moment before getting out of the car. "Is there a cover charge because I don't have any money."

"Don't worry about it," I tell her as I lead her toward the alley. "I know the band."

Brit looks uncertain, but follows me anyway. "If you're lying, I'm so kicking your ass and making you walk home."

I laugh and shoulder bump her. "You'll just have to trust me."

The alley is even worse than the front of the building. Old beer cans and cigarette butts litter the ground around the back-stage door. Standing as a lone sentry is Frank, the bouncer. He's a good six foot two and easily three hundred pounds. Someone broke his nose years ago, by the looks of it several times. He doesn't say much, just glares from his deep, recessed eyes in his acne scarred face. Not someone I ever want to get on the bad-side of. I hope he's in a good mood.

Frank scowls as we walk toward him. Brit moves near me and takes my hand. Frank is a singularly intimidating individual. If I hadn't met him before, I'm sure I would be shitting my pants in fear.

"Hey Frank. I was hoping to see Kray."

Frank glares at me and crosses his arms over his barrel chest.

Brit moves closer to me, our sides almost touching. "Maybe we should go," she whispers.

"Come on, Frank," I plead. "Kray told me to come by the side door. Could you just tell him Julius is here?"

Frank reaches up with a meaty paw and slides a toothpick between his teeth before stepping to the side and opening the door.

Taking the invitation, I pull Brit quickly up the stairs only to be stopped by Frank's thick arm.

"If'n I find out yer lyin'," Frank drawls. He doesn't finish, I've seen him manhandle drunk patrons before. If he gets mad, bad things happen.

I swallow and nod. Frank lifts his arm and I drag Brit into the cramped hallway. Brit squeezes my hand so tightly, I'm surprised it isn't broken.

We find the dressing rooms from the loud talking. I pound on the door and the voices stop.

"Who is it?" calls a voice abused by years of cigarettes.

"Kray, you better be wearing pants this time. No way I want to see your wang," I say through the closed door.

Brit gives me a shocked look and I wink back at her.

"Julius?" The door opens to Kray shirtless, but thankfully wearing pants. "What's up bro?" Kray wraps me in an alcohol and smoke-filled hug.

Kray is tall and almost painfully thin. His hair is spiked up randomly from his head with each spike sporting a different color. Tattoos cover his arms and chest, each one more disturbing than the next. Black eye-liner rings his slightly blood-shot and dilated eyes. He's floating on a sea of narcotics whose origin I've never asked about.

Kray spies Brit standing next to me and his mouth splits into a leering grin.

"You brought me a pop tart?" Kray asks, his eyes roaming over Brit. "You know I like the cherry ones the best."

Having seen a couple of his shows, I don't want to know what kind of perverse thoughts are coursing through his drug infused brain. I squelch a psychotic urge to smash my fist into his face.

"Fuck off, Kray. She's not your plaything." I can't help the low growl in my voice.

Kray arches an eyebrow at me, then his eyes dart to Brit who has moved even closer to me, her hand trembling in mine. Kray's grin widens and he chuckles a rasping sound.

"So touchy." Kray winks and walks back into the room.

I lead a hesitant Brit into the room where the other members of the band lounge while they wait for the opening act to finish. Clot, the drummer, stares off into space while he taps a rhythm on his leather-clad leg. Like the rest of the band, he's thin, shirtless, tattooed and covered in piercings. The remaining two members, Puddle and Mucus, sit hunched over their phones surfing porn, more than likely, as they pause to show the other who nods approvingly. Puddle and Mucus are twins. The only way to tell them apart is that one has blue streaks in his hair the other has red. Also, Mucus always sits on the left and Puddle on the right.

"So, you're ready for the unveiling?" Kray asks as he leans casually against the wall. I don't sit either. The chairs and couches are old and covered in things I'd rather not come in contact with.

"Yes. I hope they like it," I say.

"Like what?" Brit asks, her confidence returned now that Kray is on the other side of the room.

Kray smiles. "What? Your boyfriend didn't tell you? He made us a little present. We're showing it off tonight."

I shrug at Brit's questioning smile. "It's not that good. Just painted something for them."

What I don't say is that it took forever and I had to borrow paint from Mr. T, which I then paid back with the money that the band gave me for it.

"Alright boys," Kray says. "Let's blow this fucker up. J, you and your pop tart can watch from back stage."

Brit bristles a little at the pop tart comment now that she knows what Kray is talking about. Granted, it doesn't take much imagination. The band files out and we follow them. I hand Brit a pair of earplugs. It'll deaden the sound enough that we won't lose our hearing standing so close to the amplifiers.

"You fuckers ready for a show?" Kray screams into the microphone drowning out the roar of the packed crowd.

Kray stands there and lets it wash over him.

"Good, cuz we got somethin' to show ya!"

More cheers greet the announcement. The crowd doesn't know what's going on, but they still scream themselves hoarse.

"Check this shit out!" Kray screams as the sheet covering the back of the stage is pulled down. The crowd goes wild and my face heats. Brit stares at the Pain Splatter logo that I painted with a look of shock. I try not to see all the imperfections that I know are there. I painted it after all. The logo is painted on piece of scrap metal and bolted onto a post. I took the band name and made it look like it was splattered blood. Above the name is the stylized devil's eye that I painted on the back of my jacket. It's pretty awesome, but I can't help but see the mistakes.

"Pretty fucking badass?" Kray screams again and looks over at me. "We made up new shirts with that bad-boy on it."

The crowd roars in approval. Kray nods to me and then the band starts up. The rest of the show is a blur of loud music and Kray's screaming lyrics. I let it wash over me with Brit pressed close. At some point, someone hands me a couple shirts. I stare at the new Pain Splatter logo, my logo, emblazoned across the front. The devil's eye is repeated on the back.

In a lull in the music, Brit gives me a big hug. "It's amazing!" She half yells in my ear.

I shrug. "Um...thanks..."

After the show, I say my goodbyes to the band and drag a yawning Brit out to the car.

She digs the earplugs out of her ears. "Can you drive? I'm falling asleep on my feet."

I look at my phone, the glowing screen announcing my doom as one in the morning. "Shit. Your mom's gonna kill me."

Brit leans over my phone and looks at the time. "Oh."

"Yup."

Brit hands me the keys and we head to her house. She passes out before we leave the city. I can't help glancing at her, the highway lights playing across her face. I reach out tentatively and take her hand. Her fingers curl around mine.

It's quarter till two when I finally pull into her parent's driveway. The front porch light is off, but the rest of the house is dark. I am so going to die. Brit wakes up when the car stops. She looks down at our hands and I quickly pull mine back. She smiles sleepily at me and then yawns.

"Ok. Best get this over with," I say staring at the dark windows.

"Maybe we can sneak in without waking anyone," Brit says with another yawn.

We quietly get out. Brit waits for me to come around the car before wrapping me in another hug. Underneath the smell of cigarettes from the bar, is her clean smell of flowers.

"Thank you," she says into my hair.

I chuckle returning the hug, our bodies pressed tightly together. "Yeah, sorry about Kray. He's kind of a freak."

"That's not what I was talking about you dork," Brit says, kissing me on the cheek before breaking the hug and heads up the stairs. I try not to look at how her body moves with each step as I follow as quietly as I can.

Somehow we manage to sneak into the house without waking anyone.

"Good night, Julius," Brit whispers as she heads up the stairs to her room.

"Good night, Brit," I say equally quietly before heading downstairs.

I go to sleep, my cheek still tingling from Brit's kiss.

CHAPTER ELEVEN

It had to happen eventually. Social studies. At least I read some of the chapter, not that I remember any of it. Doesn't matter, though. What matters is that I'm going to have to deal with Mrs. Hampton and Brit. One I can't stand and the other I can't stop thinking about.

I enter class and Mrs. H gives me the hairy eyeball. I ignore her and slip into my seat. Brit is already seated and reading her notes. She doesn't even look at me. I make a point not to catch her attention. Can't help looking though. God, she's gorgeous. I force the thoughts of Brit away with the mantra you can't have her. I repeat them to myself until I stop my apparent suicidal tendencies of obsessing about her. I force my eyes forward and try and focus on the white board and its image of a pissed off Napoleon.

My phone buzzes in my pocket. I don't check. Not only would Mrs. Hampton love an excuse to take my phone, but knowing me and my grades, she'd probably work it so I have after school detention or some stupid crap like that. Not to mention the texts from Lela. I don't need read one of her "love" letters and freak out in the middle of class.

I catch Brit looking at me from the corner of my eye. Not that I'm looking at her, but still. She does look cute with her hair down and framing her heart-shaped face. Her dark eyes glitter as they bore into me. She's wearing jeans, half-boots, and a light green blouse that sets off her eyes.

What the hell am I thinking? I focus on Napoleon's scowling face and do my best to ignore her. Despite Brit's gaze on me, I manage to survive class. I even surprise everyone by remembering something from the assigned reading. Hell, Mrs. H is so surprised, she just stares at me for a moment like I'd sprouted a second head.

Class comes to an end and I breathe a sigh of relief as we all file out. Brit brushes past me without saying a word. Still, she smells amazing and the scent lingers in the air around me long after she's left.

I plaster my usual scowl on my face. Not great for making new friends, but it keeps people from bothering me. If nothing else, it cements my reputation as being a freak. Besides the jacket that is.

I squeeze through the press of bodies on the way to my locker. Only a couple minutes left to avoid another tardy, but I'm tired of lugging this damn book around and I won't need it for art class. I manage to squeak into class just as the late bell rings. It's amazing how fast you can move when you put your mind, and a couple elbows to good use.

I pull my notepad out and flip to the picture I drew the other day. I would have gotten to this earlier, but I had a clay project to finish first. I had grand plans, but it didn't work the way I wanted it to. It ended up looking like a lumpy, creepy mug. The opening has teeth and a giant deformed tongue. I'm sure it'll give some kid nightmares on open house night. The thought makes me grin a little.

I mark out a grid pattern over the picture I jotted on my notepad and then on the canvas. I start the slow process of enlarging it. It's fun to see the process in action as the tiny image becomes a larger sketch.

"Dude, that's pretty wicked," Carey says.

Carey, like the rest of us, is a little weird, but she's a good artist. Does some amazing watercolors and portraits. I wouldn't be surprised if she ended up in a gallery somewhere. The teacher is even suggesting she apply to a fancy art school. If any of us weirdos could do it, she could.

"Thanks. I hope it turns out right. Not everyone of us has a golden brush," I say, nudging her arm.

She snorts in a very unladylike manner and pushes a strand of bright purple hair out of her eyes. "Whatever, Jules. I've seen your work. You kick ass."

I shake my head. "That makes one of us. Now why don't you go draw something amazing while the rest of us losers sit over here and pretend."

Which is exactly what she does.

Carey's latest masterpiece makes me want to tear up mine and give up art for good. Only thing stopping me is she threatened to kick my ass if I even tried it. She may not be that big, but she doesn't come off as the most stable person.

By the time I leave school most of the parking lot is cleared out. I don't have to be at the body shop, so I have nowhere to be. The longer it takes to get home the less likely time I have to spend with my dad.

The wind kicks up blowing leaves sideways and making me wish I had warmer clothes. I didn't think it was supposed to be this cold, but pushing into October things get a bit dicey with the weather around here. It was supposed to be sunny and somewhat warm. Instead it's cold and cloudy. If nothing else, I would have worn a hat. I mentally flip off the weather man for getting it wrong again.

Things turn my way when I spy Brit's car sitting by itself in the parking lot. She must have an after-school thing otherwise, I'd figure she'd be home by now. Maybe it's meeting for one of the many sports she's involved in. Either way, she's still here. Which means, I might be able to bum a ride off of her.

As I draw closer, I see her huddled in the driver's seat. Something constricts in my chest. I can't explain it, but I know somethings wrong. Maybe it's the way she's sitting, I don't know. All I know is I'm jogging toward her and it has nothing to do with the cold. My heart thuds in my chest as worry pinches my gut. My only thought is to get there quickly.

My light tap on the window makes her jump, her hand clutching her jacket closed. Her hair, normally up, is loose around her shoulders. She peers at me from the corner of her eye, her face turned from me. Without saying a word, she unlocks the door. As a move around the car to the passenger side, she keeps her face turned from me and her hand tightly clutching her jacket closed.

This isn't the Brit I know. Calm. Confident. Head up. Not this. Head down and hands trembling. I try to calm my breathing and I wipe my palms on my jeans before sliding into the seat. The heat in the car is stifling after the chill outside and it takes a minute to breathe. I reach over and turn it down to level less likely to trigger spontaneous combustion.

Brit sniffs and my body stiffens. It's not the sniff of someone with a cold. I reach a tentative hand out and try to brush away the hair from her face. She shrinks from my touch and my insides turn into a block of ice. My flops uselessly back to my side.

"Brit?"

"Wh…why?" Her voice is so tiny I barely hear it.

My throat constricts and I lick my lips before answering. "What?"

"Didn't you get my text?"

My brow knits in confusion. "Text? What text?"

Brit hiccups and her hands tighten on jacket, the knuckles white. "I sent you a text." She gulps in more air, her voice shaking. "I wanted to talk to you."

"Brit. What happened?" I try to keep my voice steady despite the fear lancing through me.

"I heard footsteps and thought it was you. Most people aren't there in that part of the school after class."

Brit takes a deep, steadying breath before turning her face toward me. Every word I was going to say dies in my mouth as my throat constricts. Under one eye I see a bruise forming. The ice in my chest boils away in an inferno of rage. I close my eyes and force myself to calm down. I can't freak out.

"I called out to you…" her voice trails off and I make myself look at her. My hand moves up and pries one hand from her jacket. Her fingers are clammy, and tremors cascade down her arm. I don't need her to say who it was. I know.

"Greg." I say the name. It's not a question. I trace my thumb along her knuckles and try not to think about what it's doing to me. I focus on the reality. Greg hurt her.

"He got so mad," she continues, her voice getting quieter.

I squeeze her hand. Brit should never have been exposed to this. She's always been so full of life. To see her broken like this is too much. But I can't ignore this. This isn't like Lela. She isn't Lela.

"It's ok," I tell her as my heart breaks. "Come on. Let's get you home."

Brit shakes her head "No. I...I can't let my anyone see me like this."

"Brit..."

She turns to me and wipes tears from her eyes. That's when I see it. Red marks, like scratches, on her collar bone. I wouldn't have seen it if she hadn't let go over her jacket. I glimpse a flash of satin from her bra and immediately look away, my face heating.

Brit pulls her hand from me and I mumble an apology.

"Now you see why I can't go home?"

I nod, not trusting my voice.

"He grabbed me when I tried to leave. When I freaked about my blouse. That's when he..." she chokes back a sob.

I swivel back toward her. Before I can stop myself, my mouth is moving. "You could come over to my place. I might be able to fix it."

Confusion crawls over her face. "What?"

"I might be able to fix your shirt," I say, a blush creeping up my neck.

"I didn't know you could sew."

I shrug my shoulders and give her a weak smile. "How do you think I made the jacket?"

Her eyes widen. "I just assumed you had someone make it for you or something."

"I guess I'm full of surprises."

Brit tilts her head onto the head rest, a small smile on her lips. She lightly brushes my arm. "Thank you."

I raise an eyebrow. "Ok. Enough of the feelings stuff. I'm driving." I give her fingers a squeeze and step out of the car.

Brit joins me in front her of her car. She's still clutching her jacket closed, but she's not huddled inside. I tuck a strand of hair behind her ear, not that it helps much in this wind.

I tilt her head up so she's looking at me. "It'll be ok. I promise."

Brit's eyes slide away and she nods quickly before disappearing back into the car. With a mental sigh, I slide behind the wheel. The engine purrs to life and I give it a couple of good revs. Brit gives me a warning glare. I ignore her and peel out of the parking lot. Her shriek chases after us.

CHAPTER TWELVE

Brit glances around like a tourist taking in the old, rundown houses, and weed infested lawns of my neighborhood. I should never have brought her here. I don't know what I was thinking. It was a long fall from living next to the Thompsons to ending up in this part of town. That was back before my mom left and the Monster destroyed everything. Back when my dad could keep a job longer than a few weeks. Before I had to hide. When Brit was Blake's annoying little sister and not the beautiful girl next to me.

I slowly drive past my house and park a couple doors down. My dad's car isn't home. It's a little early for him to go to work, so he's probably lost another job and hitting the bar. Again.

I breathe a sigh of relief. Hopefully he won't be home for a while. Don't want to have to explain Brit to him. That would be an awkward conversation trying to explain a girl with a ripped blouse, and who has obviously been crying, sitting in my room.

Brit looks out the car window. "Is this your place?" she points at the house we parked in front of.

The house in question is one of the nicer ones on the block. Which isn't saying much. Larger than most and the yard hasn't completely died yet. The green paint is only a little faded. White trimming neatly boxes in the windows.

"Nah, that's Mrs. Jensen's house. Mine is a couple houses up." I wave a hand behind us.

"Why did you park here then?"

"Oh, my dad isn't home and I don't want him to accidentally hit your car." Also, I don't want him to see her car out front. If he knew it was one of the Thompson's, he'd blow a gasket. He hates them now. Not sure why.

"Your dad is that bad of a driver?" She doesn't sound convinced.

I say the only thing that comes to mind. "Only when he's been drinking."

Shocked silence. I smile at her like it's a joke. I wish it was.

I get out of the car and step into the cold afternoon air, suppressing a shiver after the warmth of the interior. Brit follows and stands next too me. She's huddled into her jacket, her hand locked on keeping it closed. I realize now why she's had to hold it closed. It's one of those ones that fastens at the bottom with a couple buttons and a belt. It looks nice, but it isn't the most functional article of clothing. I hand her keys back to her and she dumps them into her book bag.

Brit hurries to catch up to me as I walk up the hill to my house. Her reaction when we reach the house isn't what I expect. I'm waiting for the turn of her lip, any sign of derision. What I'm not expecting is her quiet acceptance. She stops just outside the gate and takes the scene in. The peeling beige paint faded to almost white. The rusted screen door swinging free in the wind. The crumbling stairs leading up to the weathered porch. There used to be a swing out front, but the chains broke and my dad never bothered to fix it. Instead he took the bench and set it on some blocks. You have to be careful when you sit on it, but nobody ever does anyway. It looks trashy, but my dad doesn't seem to mind.

The concrete path leading from the sagging porch to the front gate is broken with weeds slowly reclaiming it. The yard is small and half dead. The houses on either side crowd close against the ravages of decay and age, their gutters nearly brushing against my house. I'm grateful I'm not claustrophobic. I take Brit's elbow and guide her toward the stairs. I feel her shivering against my hand.

"What are you doing?" She asks, a slight quaver in her voice.

"The third step is loose. I don't want you falling and breaking your head open."

I lead her up the stairs and sure enough, the step shifts under her weight. I pull her tight against me to keep her from falling and the scent of her perfume fills my nose. She is so close and for a moment I don't want to let go.

"Are you ok?" Somehow I manage to keep my voice calm.

Brit nods and slowly moves away from me as she steps up onto the porch. I recover enough to fish my keys out of my pocket. It takes a couple tries but I manage to get the door unlocked. As it swings open, I'm praying that the living room isn't a complete disaster. If only I were that lucky.

It could be worse. My dad could be sitting in his boxers with a beer watching TV. The devastation that greets me is disheartening even so. What a way to introduce someone to your house. Not only does my house look like crap on the outside, but the inside looks like a liquor store exploded.

I groan in frustration as the door swings soundlessly open. None of this was here this morning. My dad has been hitting the booze hard today. A discarded paper plate with the remains of a frozen pizza glommed to it sits in the middle of the battered coffee table.

"Sorry about the mess," I mumble through clenched teeth. There are days I wish I could just smack him or leave.

"That's ok...oh!"

She couldn't see it when I was standing in the doorway, but now that I'm out of the way, the full horror of the room comes into view. Old, gray, stained carpet. Beer cans strewn about. Discarded food. Seriously disgusting. I wait for her to run screaming from the house, but she just stands there for a minute before carefully moving into the house. Her nose wrinkles at the smell of stale beer that permeates the room.

"Listen...um...I need to clean this up really quick. Why don't you go upstairs. My room is the second door on the right. In my dresser, middle drawer, are a bunch of t-shirts. Grab one. At the end of the hall is a bathroom where you can change. I'll be up as soon as I'm done." I don't wait for her to respond, I start picking up trash.

"Are you sure?" She stops and I stare at her. She bites her lower lip. "You really don't have to. I can always...um..."

"Nah, it's ok. Besides, I was an asshole the other day and you didn't deserve it." I resume picking up trash so I don't have to look at her.

"Oh." Brit heads towards the stairs. "Thank you." She says it so quiet I almost don't hear her.

I continue cleaning while I listen to her light footsteps on their stairs. Before long, I hear her enter the bathroom. I wait until I'm certain she's out of my room before I walk upstairs. I hear the faucet running. For a panicked instant, I can't remember if I cleaned the bathroom recently. Luckily, I'm the only one who uses it. My dad's room has its own bathroom.

I banish the thought from my head as I reach under my bed and drag out an old army footlocker. I found it at a garage sale, and it is the perfect size to fit all of my sewing stuff. I'm rummaging through it when Brit comes back in.

She's wearing my favorite Pain Splatter shirt. It's huge on her tiny frame. One shoulder keeps slipping down, exposing her bra strap. She's really hot and my brain starts wondering what she really looks like without my shirt. I reluctantly force the images from my head. Brit's cleaned up her mascara and done something fancy with it as I can't even tell she's been crying. The bruise is also hidden beneath layers of makeup. If I didn't know it was there, I wouldn't see it.

She stands uncertainly in the doorway, her blouse clutched in her hand. She takes in the whole room. I see her mouth tighten as her gaze pauses on the pictures above my bed. Whatever. I'm a guy. It's not like she doesn't have posters of boy bands on her wall.

"I promise I won't bite, but I can't fix your shirt if you don't hand it to me."

Her gaze swings back to me. It has to be an odd sight. Me with my long hair, faded jeans, and black shirt holding a needle and thread. At least the jacket is on the back of a chair. Less intimidating that way.

"Are you sure you can fix it?"

I give her a patient look. "I should, but I didn't get a good look at it in the car, so I'll be able to give you a better answer as soon as you give it to me."

Her cheeks color and she looks away at the mention of the open shirt incident. The bed shifts as Brit sits next to me.

"Please be careful," she says as she hands me the shirt. "It's one of my favorites."

I don't bother responding. The fabric is light in my hand. The warmth from her skin still clings to it. I catch a hint of her perfume as I turn it over in my hands. Despite the fabric being light, it didn't tear. The only damage seems to be the buttons, some are loose and the rest are missing. It should be an easy fix.

"You wouldn't happen to have the missing buttons would you." I turn and her face is inches from mine. I was so lost in the blouse, I didn't realize she was that close. Her warm breath caresses my lips before she draws back.

She shakes her head. "No. When Greg..." a pause. I see tears in her eyes.

"Ok." I forge ahead. "Since we don't have the missing buttons, that's going to complicate things. We have a couple choices."

Brit hurriedly dabs at the corner of her eyes before the tears ruin her recently repaired makeup.

"What are my choices?" Good, she's not thinking about Greg the d-bag.

"Well, I can either replace all of them with ones I have. I should have a set that will match or you find buttons to replace the missing ones."

She reaches out and runs her hand over the blouse as she chews on her lip, her brows knitted in thought. The movement shortens the distance between us and my skin prickles where it touches her. The urge to pull her close is almost overwhelming. To breathe her in. She shouldn't have this effect on me, but she does.

I hope she doesn't notice my hands shaking as her finger tips lightly brush mine. Accidental or not, it sends a jolt of lightning through me. This is insane! What am I doing? Why am I doing this? I pull a shuddering breath to and calm my nerves.

It's only been a couple seconds, but it feels like hours when she finally pulls away. My hands twitch with the desire to pull her back. Like I said, completely insane. Now that she's backed away, I can breathe again.

"Well, I'd rather it be fixed now if you have some buttons that will work." Her voice is calm. I smother my disappointment.

"Well," I clear my throat. "I think I should have something. Might take some digging."

I find the plastic container crammed full of buttons. It's full of ones I've picked up here and there. Some I bought, some I salvaged from old clothes. Most don't match, but there are a couple sets in there. When I was first teaching myself to sew, I would practice replacing and adding extra buttons. They're surprisingly easy to do and you can do some really interesting things with them. Some of the earlier designs on my jacket involved buttons, at least to map out where I wanted to put things. Only takes a couple of stitches to put them in place.

I dump the whole container out and Brit and I start sorting through them. Before too long the sorting becomes a game. Who can get the buttons first. I've never felt comfortable around girls before. It's weird, but I feel myself relaxing around her in a way that I only do with Brit. She seems to relax too, and a smile starts playing across her lips. Neither one of us mentions Greg or the bruise.

A bright blue button catches my eye at the same time she notices it. We both sit there staring at it and each other. A standoff. Gunslingers poised at high noon. Her hand darts out and snatches it just a second before mine. I grab for her and send buttons flying. With a shriek she falls back onto the bed. Before I know it, I'm on top of her, with her hands pinned above her head. Her hand is clutched firmly around the button with my hand on top. I feel the warmth of her skin through my clothes. She's breathing fast, her lips parted with a slight smile. They're so soft and inviting.

Up close I see the bruise on her cheek and reality intrudes. I pull back, the moment gone. I try to ignore the look of disappointment on her face. We can't be a thing. It would be too messy. Because even if I didn't get pummeled into oblivion by one of the men her life, she would some day learn about Lela. And then she would leave and I would be alone with my father. Again.

Brit pokes me in the forehead. "Earth, to Jules. You in there?"

I force a smile and try not to look at her cheek, or her lips. Both of which could destroy me for different reasons.

She lightly brushes her fingers on my cheek. "Are you ok?"

I choke out a laugh. Question of the century right there. Am I ok? No. Not in the slightest, but we don't have the time to get into my insanity.

"What?" Her lips turn up at the corners. She's probably trying to decide if I'm truly crazy and what force possessed her to come up to my room.

"I'm not crazy," I blurt out, my face burning.

Brit's laugh echoes through the small room, loud and bright. It eases something inside me that has been coiled tight for too long. I lay down next to her like we used to do so many years ago.

She turns and looks at me, her hands resting lightly on her stomach. "Thank you."

I cross one eye and scrunch up my eyebrows. "For what?"

"For being my friend," she says through a fit of giggles.

I ignore the sting from the f-word. I'm in the friend-zone, but at least she's smiling. And maybe for a moment she's thinking of me and not Greg. It's a long shot, but I'll take what I can get.

Her eyes close when I tuck a strand of hair behind her ear, my fingers lightly brushing her cheek. The urge to kiss her is overwhelming but I manage to cram it into its small box. I pull my hand away before I do something stupid.

"Are you going to be ok?" It's a lame question, but it's the only one I have at the moment. I'm tempted to smack myself for even saying it.

She shrinks in on herself a little, the walls closing in around her. Her fingers tighten on her stomach and she turns her head. I keep my mouth shut because honestly, I don't have anything to say. I'm out of my depth, but I'm worried. Maybe if she'll talk to me, I can convince her to dump Greg before he destroys her.

She's quiet for so long, I don't think she's going to say anything. I open my mouth to tell her to forget it. That she doesn't have to answer. She doesn't have to think. But then she starts talking.

"He's not a bad person," she says without looking at me. "Underneath everything, he's a good person. I've seen it."

CHAPTER THIRTEEN

Her words are like a punch to the gut. It dawns on me that I've said them before about Lela and my father. Underneath it all, they're good people. Or at least, they used to be. After living with them, I don't know anymore. I still say the words, but do I believe them or am I just trying to convince myself? I close the lid on that box of crazy before it overwhelms me. I need to focus on Brit and not my demons.

"When I first met him, he was...amazing." Brit pauses to take a deep breath. "He was so confident. Strong. Everyone loved him. Women wanted to be with him and guys wanted to be him."

Her breath catches and a tear rolls down her cheek. "And he was interested in me. Not them. And now..."

She trails off and I take one of her hands, unclench it, and twine my fingers with hers. Brit moves closer and I try not to think about how there is only a thin layer of cotton between us. I've dreamt about moments like this, but just us. Not with the specters of my dad or Greg hanging over our heads.

"And now I don't know what to do."

I give her hand a squeeze. "It'll be ok. We'll figure something out."

She turns towards me, a small smile tugging at her lips. "Thank you."

I shrug it off. "What are friends for?" The words burn my mouth.

She doesn't miss a beat. "Hiding bodies?" Her smile trembles as she tries to keep from laughing. It's an old joke, but still a funny one and it breaks my sullen thoughts.

With a wicked grin, I poke her in the ribs. Brit shrieks before dissolving into laughter. The laughter does her good, her eyes brighten, her face is flushed. She's never looked more beautiful. She bites her lip, a huge grin on her face.

Brit's phone chimes, breaking the moment. She sits up, her eyes wide. With a trembling hand, she pulls her cell out of her purse. I'm hoping it isn't Greg. That's the last thing she needs. Brit heaves a sigh of relief.

"It's my parents. I have to go."

"I hope you aren't in trouble."

She shakes her head. "Yes and no. I've been in worse."

I raise an eyebrow. "You've been in trouble? I thought you were perfect."

Brit gives me a look and then ruins it by sticking out her tongue. She reaches for her torn blouse. "What should I do about this?"

I sit up and take it from her. "Don't worry about it. I'll get it fixed and I'll bring it over sometime."

Brit tenses.

"When your parents aren't home. Promise."

She gives me a relieved smile. "Walk me to my car?" she asks, holding out her hand.

I roll my eyes. "Fine." I draw the word out and let out a fake grunt as I stand up. "So demanding." I smile and take her hand. Without even trying, our fingers lace together. My heart stutters and I hope she can't feel it. I'm her friend, I remind myself.

We're halfway down the stairs when the kitchen door bangs open. I freeze, causing Brit to bump into me.

"What's..."

I wave her quiet and mouth "My dad."

"Woo!" He calls out. "It sure is cold out there." His voice is heavy with alcohol.

"Oh Frankie," a female voice coos. "I know how to keep you

warm."

"I bet you do," my father replies.

The female voice giggles.

I force the queasy feeling down. My father has a new girlfriend, at least for the evening. And Brit is here. If it were possible for my face to spontaneously combust from embarrassment, I'm sure I would be engulfed in flames. The drunk kissing noises from the other room are enough to turn my stomach. I hate this part. The upside to all this is that they are too engrossed in each other to notice us sneaking out the front door.

"Oh hey there, Jules," my dad slurs.

Or maybe not. I force my face into a neutral expression before turning to face him. "Oh hey, dad. Didn't expect you home so early."

He gives me a sheepish grin. Which turns wolfish when he spies Brit. "Well," he says drawing out the word. "Miranda and I were just wanting to spend some time getting to know each other." His eyes rove over Brit the entire time he's talking.

Miranda giggles, oblivious to the fact my father is not even looking at her. I try not to vomit.

I glance at them. She's draped over him, a half-drunken smile on her overly red lips. "Hi." I give a half-wave. "We were just leaving." I start moving toward the door, Brit in tow.

"No need to rush off," my dad says. Brit's hand tightens in mine. She's noticed his gaze too. "You haven't introduced your friend."

Bile pushes its way up my throat. "Her name's..." I pause. If I tell him her real name, he'll know who she is. Ever since mom left, he's blamed the Thompsons. I doubt they had anything to do with it. Besides, she left because of my dad. She left me here because I wasn't good enough.

"Renea," Brit fills in the gap. "We go to school together."

I breathe an inward sigh of relief. I didn't know she could lie that well. Granted she's been dating Greg without anyone knowing, so maybe there's more to her than I thought.

"It's a pleasure to meet you, Renea." My father's entire bearing has shifted from sloppy drunk to predatory. "Please, don't let us make you feel like you have to leave."

His sudden interest in Brit is not lost on Miranda either, who glares daggers at us. It dawns on me that neither my father, nor Miranda, are as drunk as they seem. I almost laugh at the absurdity of it all. Both feigning inebriation to get the other one in bed. What isn't silly is my father's reaction to Brit. Although he's still standing in the kitchen, his arms around Miranda, his presence has slithered into the room with us. I want to bathe in bleach.

"Actually, she has to get home." Miranda's face relaxes at my announcement. "I was just walking her to her car."

"Okay then," my dad says with a big smile. "Maybe next time. It was nice meeting you, Renea."

Brit smiles weakly, her hand trembling in mine, as she follows me toward the door and safety.

"See you around," my dad calls out.

I wave without looking and we step out into the chilly evening. "That was…"

"Weird," I interrupt her with a pained smile. "I'm really sorry."

Brit shakes her head. "It's ok."

I can tell it really bothered her, but she doesn't want to hurt my feelings or something like that. I slip my arm around her and give her a side hug.

"No. It isn't ok. He was being…" I pause searching for a word. "Creepy?"

I snort. "Yeah. He was. Sorry."

Brit stops. "No. Don't apologize for him." She looks up at me. "Just don't."

I look at her, emotions warring inside me. I shouldn't apologize for him, but at the same time, I feel like I have to.

"I'm sorry." It's lame. I'm lame.

Brit puts a finger to my lips and the world stops as I am overwhelmed with the urge to kiss it. She must be thinking the same thing because her face turns pink and she quickly pulls her hand away.

"If you need anything, buttons or something. Let me know. I'll get them. Okay?" The change in topic saves us both from the awkward moment.

I nod, my lips still tingling from the touch of her finger.

She smiles. "I trust you."

There's hidden meaning behind her words. Or at least I think there is. My brain churns with an appropriate response as we walk up to her car.

"That makes four of us," I say with a smile.

Her forehead crinkles in confusion. "What?"

"Sorry. Random. I was going to say something, but realized it sounded stupid."

Brit giggles as we step up to her car. She opens her door and flashes a beaming smile at me. "Thank you."

It's my turn to be confused. "For what?"

"For being you," she says and gives me a quick hug.

But I'm nobody. I'm nothing. Those words never get said as she drives off leaving me alone in the street.

By the time I get back inside, my dad and his girlfriend for the evening have disappeared into his room. Already noises are emanating that I try not to think about too much. My phone buzzes. Thinking it's Brit, I look. It isn't.

Lela: I miss you, baby. Call me.

It's too much. Disappearing into the kitchen, I notice an open beer can resting on the counter. I don't even think, I just grab it and pour its bitter contents down my throat. It makes me feel a little queasy, but after a couple minutes, I don't care anymore. I don't care about anything. The gross sounds my dad and his date are making, don't bother me. Lela texting me? Nothing. I don't even care about being a loser. A second can follows the first.

CHAPTER FOURTEEN

I stumble upstairs sometime around midnight. The world tilts and shifts and it's hard to focus. I'm pretty sure I hid the cans. He shouldn't notice anyway. Can't be too certain. I don't know how my father functions like this. With each step my stomach wants to forcibly evict its contents. It takes all my willpower not to hurl all over the carpet.

Finally, I make it to my bedroom. Maybe if I lie down the world will stop spinning. Drinking doesn't make Brit's rejection any easier. I don't know why people even say it does. I crash into my bed with a groan. The world wobbles a few times before settling. If I don't breathe too hard, I should survive.

My sheets smell like Brit. I gather them up to my nose and breathe deeply. Her perfume infuses my brain. My lips tingle at the memory of the kiss, so innocent and tender. My heart races at the memory. I tumble into sleep with her scent filling me.

The dreams start, as they always do, but this time distorted by alcohol and Brit's rejection. It starts with blood on the linoleum. So hard to clean up. Lela is crying the whole time and no matter how much I scrub, it never goes away. Bloody lips touching mine. I don't want to remember Lela like this. Sweet. Gentle. Caring. Lela crawling into bed next to me, putting her bruised cheek against my neck. Her tears mixing with the blood and soaking my pillow. She clings to me, desperate for comfort. She kisses me on the neck, and I try to push her away, but she won't let go.

I wake with a gasp, my stomach roiling. I sprint to the bathroom, slam open the toilet and vomit. Beer and bile mix with the water. My dreams are usually nightmares, but it has been a while since I dreamed of Lela. Maybe it's Brit. Maybe it's the beer. Maybe both. Miranda moving in with us definitely plays a part in it.

I lean my cheek on the cool linoleum as my stomach finally settles. Images of Lela threaten to overwhelm me. I curl into a ball with a groan. My head is pounding and I'm drenched in sweat. I wonder if I'm going to die like this, lying on the floor of the bathroom. A fitting end for a pathetic loser like me.

I wish I could die and let the pain go. It's not the first time I've felt that way. Been a while since the thoughts have been this strong. They started when I was fourteen, when Lela first started living with us. When she first started crawling into my bed crying after my father passed out for the night. At first, I felt important. I felt like I was helping her. Then the guilt, the shame, started worming its way into my mind. It was wrong that she was with me. I knew that, but I wanted to help. I was making her feel better. Giving her a place where she wasn't threatened. A place where she could be comforted and happy before diving back into the sea of madness that is the Monster.

I never told anyone, not even Blake. It's my private shame.

I manage to crawl up to a sitting position. I move slowly in case my stomach decides to rebel again. It gives a tentative gurgle, but nothing explosive. I drag myself to my feet, flush the toilet, then stumble over to the sink. My mouth tastes like a sewer. I rinse it, then brush my teeth multiple times before stumbling back to bed. I curl up in bed and suppress a whimper as my head threatens to explode.

I doubt I'll sleep. I wish I could. It would mean I wouldn't feel the pounding in my skull. On the other hand, with sleep comes the dreams. Feeling like crap outweighs memories of Lela and her broken love.

The glowing face of my alarm clock say the time is 1:15. It's going to be a long miserable night. I pull the sheets back up to my nose. I smell only sweat and fear. All traces of Brit have been obliterated by my nightmare. My thoughts skitter through my head as I desperately look for sleep.

I force the memories of Lela back into their box where they belong. It's a struggle, but I manage to do it. I imagine I'm painting a car by hand. Each brush stroke hides another memory. Before long she's secure behind layers of paint and sealant, the surface perfectly smooth.

I tumble back into sleep and oblivion.

The shrill screech of the alarm clock shatters my restless sleep and pierces my skull like nails. By the time I smash my hand over the snooze button, I have a screaming headache. My eyes are crusted shut with sleep and tears.

I manage to pry them open and make sense of the world. My head feels fuzzy and my stomach flips in protest. Somehow I manage to crawl out of bed and shamble to the bathroom. I'm hoping a shower will clear my brain enough that I can make it to school. I don't want to stay home. I'd rather go to school half dead then deal with my father.

The water is like hot needles on my face, but at least it clears my head enough that I can make it to school. What happens after that is anyone's guess. I'll deal with school when I get there. I down some aspirin with a grimace using a cold glass of water to wash out the chalky feeling in the back of my throat.

The thought of food makes my stomach uneasy, but I manage to choke down some cereal and toss a cup of coffee from yesterday's pot into the microwave. I'm taking my chances with drinking the stuff, but I need to wake up.

I open the fridge and have to force down bile when I see the beer on the shelf. I slam the door shut and lean my head against the cool metal. I breathe slowly and deeply until my stomach settles. Never again. It's a solemn vow. I am never touching that stuff again. Not only does it taste terrible, but the thought of it sliding down my throat makes me want to puke.

Once I convince myself I won't die, I grab my jacket and backpack. I realize I didn't get Brit's blouse fixed. Crap. I'll have to talk to her and apologize. I can imagine the look of disappointment and betrayal on her face. I promised and failed. It's simple enough to fix too.

I stumble out my front door and head toward school. The cold breeze knifes through my open jacket. I shiver and pull it closed. The sky is cloudy and gray. The leaves have changed and litter the ground in red and orange piles. It won't be long before it gets really cold and my morning commute will get miserable.

I trudge through the dying landscape. The clock on my phone says that I have just enough time to get to school. I just want to curl up into a ball and sleep for a week. I shiver and huddle further into my jacket.

Thoughts of Brit once again float in my head. Her face swirls mixing with other pictures in my head. Lela rises to the surface again and my step falters before the door slams shut on it. I force myself to focus on happier images. Goofing off with Brit, painting cars, hanging out with Blake, watching old 80's action shows with Mr. T. I flip through them like a photo album, never settling long on any moment. Every time I stop, Lela floats up and merges with Miranda.

I wonder how long it will be before Miranda crawls into bed with me after suffering at the hands of the Monster. How long before she seeks comfort and clings to me. How long before I find her curled up on the bathroom floor crying and bleeding, telling me she has to leave and will I please help her.

I know all these things will happen. I'll hold her and then help her gather up her few possessions and watch her drive away. By the time he wakes up, she'll be gone. The Monster will rage at its lost victim. I'll be ready this time. I'll make sure I can get to my room or out the front door. He won't catch me, won't hurt me like last time, won't leave me bleeding on the floor. He won't be able to stand over my broken and bleeding body, a triumphant curl to his lip.

A truck drives by and honks, causing me to jump. I catch a

glimpse of Greg's laughing face as he speeds down the street. My blood boils with the shame of showing weakness. I know he'll laugh and point out the big sissy to his friends.

I shiver as the cold wind buffets against me. I turn up my collar and continue my trek to school. The walk is long, cold, and lonely. If I don't die before I get to school, I'll be amazed. My nose clogs up and starts to run. It would be just my luck to get sick on top of everything else. My life sucks.

CHAPTER FIFTEEN

By the time I make it to my locker, I feel like I'm going to puke.

I should have stayed home, slept it off, but at some point my dad is going to wake up and I'd have to deal with him. School, even hung-over and dying of the plague, is preferable to dealing with my father.

The final bell rings and I realize I've been staring at my open locker the whole passing period. Maybe I should go to the nurse. Lie down. Get some aspirin. It means missing Chemistry, but at the moment, I don't care.

I stumble down the hallway toward the nurse's office. At least, I think I'm headed in the right direction. I lean my head against the cool tile of the wall. It clears the fog enough so that I can orient myself. Now if the hall would stop spinning I would be happy.

"Julius?" Someone calls out. I recognize the voice, but my brain is mostly non-functional at this point. "Julius? Are you ok?"

Finally it clicks. "Oh hi, Brit," I mumble. "What are you doing out of class?"

"What? Oh, I had..." she pauses as she touches my forehead. "Wow, you're burning up. We need to get you to the nurse's office."

And here I thought it was just a hangover, guess I'm wrong. Luckily Brit is athletic and can easily handle my weight as I lean against her.

"Brit," I manage through clenched teeth. "You smell funny."

She barely manages to keep from dropping me when she stumbles.

"What do you mean I smell funny," she asks.

"Dunno," I manage to get out. "Just weird."

"Well, you're high because I smell just like me." She rearranges my head so it's not buried in her neck anymore. The smell clings to her like perfume. Then it clicks.

"You're wearing perfume?" I ask as we drunkenly stumble down the hall.

Brit sighs. "If you make fun of me, I'm dropping you right here."

I groan. "You'll drop me anyway when I barf on your shoes."

Brit pokes me in the ribs. "You're a real ass when you're sick."

"Sorry," I say unapologetically. "It's part of my charm." I smile weakly.

Brit grunts. "Doesn't change that you're an ass."

By the time we manage to make it to the nurse's office, my legs feel like rubber. My head is throbbing, my teeth are chattering so hard I'm sure people can hear it over the marching band. On the upside, I don't want to hurl anymore. I do however want to die, or eat someone's brains.

"Braaaaains," I groan.

Brit starts to laugh and almost drops me on the floor. Our feet tangle and we both land on the bed. She lands on top of me, her face inches from mine, her eyes wide. Brit hurriedly gets up, her cheeks pink. She quickly looks away and smooths her clothes as the nurse comes over.

"What seems to be the problem?" the nurse asks.

"He's not feeling well," Brit says, saving me from having to explain.

I get comfortable on the cot and the nurse runs a thermometer across my forehead.

"101," she clucks. "We'll have to contact your parents and get you home."

"Don't," I manage to croak out.

I hear the nurse huff in frustration. "And why not, young man?"

I scour my fevered brain for a reason. Telling her I don't want to go home because I'll have to deal with the Monster isn't an option.

"His dad works nights and their car is broken down."

The lie rolls off Brit's tongue flawlessly. I'm impressed, didn't think she could do that. I crack open an eye and give her a weak smile of appreciation before rolling over.

"Thank you for bringing him here, Brittany," the nurse says. "Now, get back to class."

I hear the crinkle of paper as the nurse hands Brit a hall pass. I feel a pat on my hip.

"I'll see ya later, Jules. If you need a ride after school, just let me know and I'll call Blake. K?"

Even dealing with a pathetic lump like me, Brit is still nice. Definitely don't deserve this kind of treatment.

I groan as I curl up shivering under the blanket the nurse drapes over me. I hear the nurse moving around and then a cold pack is placed on my boiling forehead. It feels heavenly and I sigh as it cools my fevered brain. After that she leaves me alone.

I pass in and out of consciousness for the next several hours. Sometimes I hear the nurse talking to students and sometimes she's tapping at her computer keyboard. Except for changing the cool pack on my head, she doesn't interact with me, which suits me just fine as I feel like ass.

I feel a pressure on my back. Someone is leaning against me and an arm is resting on mine. Fingers stroke my shoulder in little circles. It's a nice sensation, soothing. I snuggle deeper into the blankets. Eventually curiosity gets the better of me and I peek out from my blanket cocoon. Brit smiles tentatively, her hazel eyes sparkling.

"Go away," I groan as I pull the blanket over my head.

There is no way I'm dealing with her right now. Hell, it's her fault I'm in this condition. Except it isn't. It's my fault. I got drunk on my own.

Brit sighs in frustration and pulls the blanket from my head. I try to stop her, but I'm too weak. God, I hate being sick.

"I'm sorry." She says it so quiet yet it pulls at my heart. "School's done for the day. Time to go home."

I don't want her to be sorry. I want her to go away and leave me alone. I don't deserve someone like her in my life, especially someone that I want to kiss so badly. I remember her soft lips, her perfume filling me. She broke something inside of me with that kiss. I don't know what it is, but I can't think when she's around and I can't live when she isn't.

Anger bubbles underneath and I latch on to it like a drowning man. Hoping it will pull me up, save me from her, but it doesn't. I'm drowning and I'm doing it willingly because she wants me to.

"You ready to go?" Her hazel eyes snag me again and I'm back to last night. It takes my breath away.

"Yeah," I grumble. Brit helps me stand up. The world doesn't spin as much. My head pulses only a little, not nearly as bad as earlier that day. I smile thanks to the nurse as I shuffle out the door.

I better not be sick. Don't want to end up spending the day at home. I'm a moron for drinking that much last night. A spike of fear pierces my chest. I hope I hid the cans. My dad knows I clean up after him and I'm a horrible liar.

Brit and I walk slowly out to her car. The parking lot is emptying as students scurry everywhere but the school. It's a mass exodus of cars honking and swerving to avoid collisions. I'm glad I don't drive. I'd die in a fiery crash or something lame like that.

A large engine purrs up behind us and revs. I cast a glance behind us and I see Greg glaring at me from behind the wheel of his truck. It fits his ego. It's huge. The bright red paint is almost painful to look at. The truck is completely impractical, but I doubt Greg cares. The way he's looking at me, I'm sure he'd like to introduce me to the dual rear tires in back. The personalized plate tops the whole thing off. 55Crush. His number and nickname. Definite massive ego there.

Without thinking, I let my fingers catch Brit's as our arms swing in counterpoint to our steps. For a moment, they swing in unison before Brit quickly pulls her hand away. She gives me a warning glare, but the damage is done. I hear the heavy thump of Greg's truck door slam shut.

I spin around in time for him to plant his meaty hands square in my chest and shove me to the ground. I land painfully on my shoulder, the jacket taking most the impact. Still hurts, but at least I don't get road rash with it.

I sit there for a second, dazed. I clear my head in time to see Greg yank Brit around to face him. She cries out as he pulls her inches from his face. His eyes bulge and veins protrude from his neck. I see movement out of the corner of my eye as students stop to watch.

"What the hell was that all about?" Greg screams, spittle flying from his mouth.

The watching students shift uncontrollably, but nobody moves to stop him. They're scared of him and for good reason.

Brit tries to back away from him despite his hand gripping her arm. She's so terrified of him that she can't even speak. I know that feeling too well. A pressure starts building in my chest. A rage like nothing I've felt before.

"Dammit! Answer me! Are you cheating on me with that piece of trash?!" More spittle flies onto Brit's face.

Her head swivels toward me, her pupils dilated, her body trembling. The pressure builds even more until it feels like my chest is going to explode. Greg shakes her to get her attention. More students have joined the ring, but nobody is stopping him. They are all afraid like me.

The pressure turns to anger, boiling and burning away my fear. I will not let him hurt her. She's too nice, too innocent, too pure. With a roar I spring to my feet. The whole world slows down. Greg's head starts to turn toward me, a look of stupid shock on his face. In his entire life, I doubt anyone has stood up to him.

I throw my entire body into him. I don't even think about the fact that he could crush me in a second. My mind is empty of thought. In its place is a searing rage that wants nothing more than to smash his head into the side of his truck. Which is exactly what I do. The door dents slightly from the impact and Greg slumps to the ground, his eyes rolling back. He's unconscious, but I don't care.

I fall on him and send my fists pummeling. I no longer have control, it isn't me anymore. It's a Monster, just like my father's. I feel hands grabbing at me and I shove them away with a snarl. More hands grab me and force me back. I yell and scream, straining against the human cage keeping me from my prey.

I hear someone calling my name, pleading with me. The voice is high-pitched, familiar. I look around, searching for it, but all I see are faceless people holding me, their features distorted by the wall of rage burning inside me. I strain against them, but they've moved me too far away from Greg. The Monster slowly loosens its hold on me and my body slumps in exhaustion.

The students release me and I crash to the ground, gasping for air. They stand between me and Greg like a shield, but it doesn't matter. The rage has left me weak and trembling as the adrenaline stops pumping through my system. The fever slams back into my consciousness.

I hear my name being called and I look over at Brit. There are scratches on her face, her mascara ruined by the tears flowing down her cheeks. I reach for her, but she shrinks back. I curl up in a ball on the cold cement as I realize what has happened, what I've done. I've let the Monster out of the cage. I'm worthless, I'm an animal.

Just like my father.

Strong hands pull me to my feet and I don't resist as the SRO and two other male teachers march me into the school. I look at Brit one last time. She looks away. It's over. My one shot at happiness and I blew it. I'm such a worthless piece of crap.

CHAPTER SIXTEEN

Everyone stops and stares when they see the SRO and the teachers escorting me to the office. News of my altercation in the parking lot hasn't traveled this far yet. That won't be the case for long. By tomorrow the whole school will be buzzing about it.

The rumor mill will get a hold of it, and then all sorts of permutations will spin down the halls. Of course, I won't be around to hear it. If I am lucky, I'll only be gone a week or two. Worst case, is expulsion. I'm guessing on expulsion. Dr. Stevens doesn't think too highly of me, for good reason.

I'm nothing.

We stop in front of her office. She must have been expecting us because I am ushered in without a knock. I catch a glimpse of a pale, and shaken Brit going into another office as I enter Dr. Stevens' domain. She glances at me before the door closes, blocking her from sight.

I slump into the chair in front the desk with the school resource officer flanking me. My other two escorts leave once I'm seated. Dr. Stevens' stares at me over the rim of her glasses. I can see her weighing my sins and finding me wanting.

I can't keep her gaze for long and I drop my eyes and stare at my hands. Defeated. Lost. Alone. There is nothing I can say to change the outcome, so I keep silent.

If I died right now, she'd dance on my grave.

"Thank you, Jon," Dr. Stevens' says, addressing the SRO. "I

think we'll be fine here."

"Sure thing," replies Jon in his deep voice. "Holler if you need anything." I hear the door open and his heavy steps exit the room.

The voice fits him. He's a large black man, bald, heavy-set with hands bigger than my head. His piercing almost black eyes can bore into even the toughest ganger. All he has to do is lay one of his meaty paws on your shoulder and you tell him everything.

He used to be a cop, but he retired and decided to work at our school. Rumor mill says a lot about his retirement, most of it bad, but nobody dares say it to his face. I'm sure he knows what is said, but leaves it alone. The more kids fear him, the less likely they are to cause trouble.

Despite his menacing demeanor toward troublemakers, he doesn't have a mean bone in his body. He smiles pleasantly at teachers and students, all the while watching everything. Despite my many trips to the office, this is the first time he's escorted me.

Dr. Stevens' sighs and I hear her glasses clink against her desk. I glance up and watch her rub her hands over her face. She looks tired. I guess dealing with me would wear anybody out. Maybe that's why my mom left. Maybe it wasn't the Monster. It was me.

"Julius." She says my name with a note of disappointment. "What happened? You were doing so well. Attending classes, getting your homework in, and now this?"

I look down at her hands, I can't bear to look at her anymore. There's nothing to say, so I shrug my shoulders. She wouldn't believe me even if I told her the truth. Besides, I just beat the crap out of the star football player.

"Julius, if you don't tell me what happened, I won't have much choice in what action I take."

I don't say anything. I know I messed up bad. The moment I looked in Brit's eyes, I knew just how bad I fucked up. She saw the Monster. I'm no better than my father.

Dr. Stevens lets out a frustrated breath. "Ok, listen. I'm going to have the SRO sit with you while I go talk to a few of the other students. You think about what I said. You do have a choice,

Julius."

I watch out of the corner of my eye as she heads toward the door. Jon walks back into the office, grabs a nearby chair and spins it around so he can face me while resting his arms across the top of the back. I look away before I meet his eyes. I don't want to see the disappointment in them.

"You messed up Greg pretty good." His voice rumbles in his chest when he speaks.

I don't respond. There's no need, he knows what I did.

"He was awake and standing by the time the paramedics got there."

His words, said in their calm measured way, start shredding my defenses. My eyes burn with unshed tears. Greg's a bully, but paramedics? I remember my daydream about him lying broken on the ground. I remember being happy in the dream. Now, I just feel hollow.

"He'll be ok. Probably just a concussion, maybe a couple stitches. He'll miss a few games at most, I'm sure."

Each word slams into me. The tears start running. I want them to stop, but I can't. I feel ashamed, worthless. Jon just sits there watching me cry.

"He must have made you real mad for you to do that to him."

I crack. I tell him about Greg grabbing me in the hallway, about Brit and her torn blouse, about the parking lot. The words keep pouring out and the tears flow. I slam the door in my head before I tell him about the Monster.

Jon sits quietly listening. He's broken me. He heaves himself up from the chair with a quiet groan and grabs a tissue out of the box on Dr. Stevens desk. He hands it to me before heading to the door without another word. I sit there wiping up the tears and snot while I await my fate. Eventually, Dr. Stevens returns and sits behind her desk.

"Ok, Julius," she says as she pulls out some papers. "We called your house, but nobody answered. Do you know where your father might be?"

"No," I say in a quiet monotone.

"Ok. Do you need a ride home?"

"No," I reply again.

"Here's what's going to happen. We have a zero tolerance policy for physical confrontations on school grounds. As such, I am forced to suspend you for one week, out of school."

She pushes a piece of paper toward me.

"You'll need to have your parents sign this form before you can return to school. You will be responsible for making up any missed homework. Understand?"

I nod my head.

"Julius, look at me."

I raise my eyes without moving my head.

"If this happens again, you will be expelled, and you will have to repeat your senior year. Understand."

"Yes." My voice is small. I'm small, worthless, stupid. All the what ifs bounce around in my head like a pinball machine.

"Ok, you're dismissed. Go home."

I slowly stand up and shuffle out the door, the piece of paper clutched in my hand. Somehow I managed not to get expelled. I don't know how it happened, or why, but none of that matters. I'm still a failure. Still my own Monster.

Brit isn't around when I finally leave the office. The school's deserted except for a few stragglers.

The parking lot is empty by the time I return to the scene of my crime. Greg's truck is still there, but somebody took the time to park it. I don't want to look, but I can't help myself. If I see the dent, it will be real. I won't be able to hide from it.

The damage isn't as large as I imagined it would be. I kneel down and gaze at it. Memorize the shape. A spot of blood marks the center like a bullseye. I could have killed him. If people hadn't stopped me, I might have. I'm not a big guy, but he wasn't able to defend himself.

There is no sense of triumph, only shame. I'm worthless and stupid for letting myself hurt Greg. Doesn't matter that he's an asshole or that he messes with everyone he feels is weaker. I assaulted him. I could have waited. The teachers would have come. I'm sure they saw the whole thing on the cameras. Heaving myself up, I turn away from the evidence of my sin.

I have no idea where I should go, so I let my feet take me where they want. The trees are beautiful this time of year and I try to banish thoughts of Greg from my mind by focusing on them. It doesn't work. I still see him grabbing Brit, still feel his body go slack when I slam his head into the door. My stomach rolls and I force the bile down. The fever clouds my thoughts.

Before I notice it, I'm standing in front of my house. Somehow my feet knew where to go, where all monsters belong. The autumn air nips at my ears and nose. The lights are on. My father's home. I notice an unfamiliar car in the driveway. It must be Miranda's. Nobody else comes by our house.

I push open the door to smell of delicious food coming from the kitchen. I'm not sure what it is, but my mouth waters. I hear my father talking as pots and pans are shuffled around on the stove. It's a surprisingly domestic sound for our house. Usually food is just grabbed as an afterthought, a necessity. The less time spent in the kitchen the better.

"Is that you, Julius?" my father calls out.

"Yeah," I reply as I head toward the stairs and my sanctuary.

My father comes out of the kitchen, a white towel draped over his shoulder. My father's forehead crinkles and moves quickly over and peers into my face.

"Are you ok?" He asks, his hand lightly resting on my shoulder.

"No, I feel like crap. Spent most of the day in the nurse's office."

He puts a hand to my head. It's a surprisingly gentle touch and my eyes burn with the threat of tears.

"Why didn't you have the school call? I would have picked you up."

I shrug. "I figured you were asleep and I didn't want to wake you."

My father's cheeks turn slightly pink. "Oh yeah, well, we've

been up for a while. We went to the store and got a few things."
My father rolls his eyes, a smile playing on his lips. "Miranda
seems to think that we weren't getting a healthy diet."

I smile weakly. Nutritional health is the least of my concerns
these days. I dread telling him about Greg, but he'll find out soon
enough.

"Did you get a call from the school this afternoon?" I ask. It's
best to get these things over with. The longer I wait the worse it
will be.

My father looks confused for a second. "No. Miranda and I
were at the store. Why?"

I force myself to look my father in the eye. "I got into a fight
today."

My father stills and my gut clenches.

"What happened?" he asks, his hands clenching.

I tell him, about Greg, about everything that happened. I don't
gloss over it. I don't hesitate. My father stands quietly. When I
get to the part where Greg pinned me up against the locker, his
jaw clenches. When I finish, my father is smiling. I stop and look
at him with a confused look.

"I'm proud of you son," he says as he claps me on the back.
"You really showed that asshole to never mess you again."

"But I got suspended," I'm shocked. I don't remember the last
time he said he was proud of me.

My father shrugs. "The schools are run by dicks. They should
have given you a goddamn medal."

I nod in agreement, I don't trust myself to lie and pretend to
agree with him.

"Why don't you go lay down. I'll have Miranda bring you
some dinner in a bit." My father squeezes my arm slightly as he
walks back into the kitchen.

I do feel like crap. Lying down sounds like a good idea. I
shuffle upstairs to my room. Despite my father's praise, I still feel
the weight of guilt pressing on my soul. I curl up in my bed as the
shivers start again. I curse myself for not calling for a ride. The
walk home didn't do the fever any favors. Maybe if I'm lucky I'll

catch pneumonia.

My teeth are chattering by the time Miranda brings dinner up. She looks at me with a mixture of uncertainty and concern before she sets a plate covered with roast beef, mashed potatoes, and corn on my on my bedside table with a cup of hot tea. If I felt better, I would enjoy the delicious smells. As it is, I lay there dying.

It takes a Herculean effort, but I manage to drag the plate onto my bed. It tastes as good as it smells. The warmth of the food spreads through me and banishes some of the chill. I eat as much as I can before I get too sleepy and oblivion claims me.

CHAPTER SEVENTEEN

I spend the next couple days sleeping. I don't remember the last time I did something like that. It's nice not to have to worry about the Monster, even if it is temporary.

Blake calls me to ask how I'm doing. I grumble something about feeling like death warmed over and go back to sleep. I'm sure he's heard from Brit that I got suspended, but he doesn't mention it when he calls. It will come up eventually, but I'm not in the mood to go over it with him.

Miranda doesn't say much, just leaves me food at regular intervals before leaving. I try not to encourage any connection between us. Not only is her existence in my life temporary, I don't want another Lela.

Once I stop feeling like a zombie, I manage to crawl out of bed. Not only do I need a shower, but I can't stop thinking about Brit. I need to talk to her. I need to know if she hates me. If nothing else, I need to apologize for scaring her. I didn't mean to. I just got mad. I hope she understands.

It's amazing how good a shower feels after being sick. The water cleanses me. I make a mental note to change my bed. Don't want to crawl back into the viral cocktail that has brewed in my sheets.

Feeling refreshed, I pull on some fresh clothes. There's no sign of Miranda or my dad moving around. It seems I have the house to myself for the next several hours until school lets out.

I should fix Brit's shirt as a peace offering. I did promise to fix it. She never picked out buttons, but I know I've got something that should look good on it. I walk back upstairs and drag my sewing box out and run my fingers over the old wood of the footlocker. It wasn't that long ago that Brit and I were sorting through the assorted fasteners. Feels like forever.

I push away the sadness and focus on finding a matching set of buttons. It takes a good half hour, but I find some in a cream color. They're about the same size as the original ones, so they should work. I need to take my time. I want it perfect. Lining all the buttons up is the delicate part. The rest is just making sure the threads are enough to keep it from pulling out.

My phone rings before I'm done. It's not a number I recognize. "Hello?"

"Julius?" Brit's voice is hesitant on the other line.

"Yeah."

"I…uh…could you come over?"

The uncertainty wrenches at my heart. She sounds scared. Considering what I did to her boyfriend, I don't blame her. But she wants to see me, the least I can do is try to make things better.

"Sure."

The shirt isn't done so I set it aside to deal with it later. There is still a bunch to do and not enough time to do it in. Instead, I fold it gently and lay it flat inside the sewing box. I lock my bedroom door and step outside. Winter seems to be taking over, the air is cold and crisp. I'll need to break out the winter coat soon. Turning towards Brit's house, I start the long walk. I run through the various things I could say and her, probably negative, responses. In my fantasy, she jumps into my arms and kisses me passionately. Those thoughts alone keep me warm despite the biting cold.

And here I am again. Standing in front of another door. Building up the courage to open it. Story of my life.

Brit's house makes mine look like a rotting pile of crap. Where mine is rundown and old, hers is large and modern. The yard is huge and not mostly weeds like mine. This place feels like home and not home at the same time.

The door opens before I can knock. Brit stares at me, anger etched across her perfect features. Her arms are crossed. My brain implodes as my carefully planned apology bursts into flames. She's beautiful and imposing and clearly not amused at my silence.

"Sorry it took so long," I say, staring at my shoes.

I look up at her from under my eyelashes. And I watch her anger melt.

"It's ok," she says taking my hand. "I'm sorry, I just had a rotten day."

Electricity runs up my arm and kick starts my heart into high gear. I want nothing more than to pull her into my arms and kiss her. She's close enough. All I would have to do is take one step. One tiny step.

"You wanted to see me?" I ask forcing my voice calm.

"Oh, yeah. Sorry," Brit says looking down.

When she looks up at me again, her eyes are bright with tears.

"I…" she stumbles over the words. "Greg and I broke up and I…I didn't want to be alone right now."

"I'm sorry," I say touching her cheek gently.

Brit presses her face into my hand as tears fall onto my fingers.

"Don't be sorry," she says sadly. "Please, don't be sorry."

My feet move and suddenly I'm inches from her. Her lips part slightly and the vein in her throat jumps under her skin with each beat of her heart. I entwine my fingers with hers as I put my arm around her waist, drawing her closer to me. Her tongue darts across her lips and I can't stop myself. I capture her lips with mine. She shudders and presses into me as our lips match rhythm.

I pull her even closer as I lose myself in the kiss. Everything fades away except for her, her lips, her body pressed against mine. The chill air evaporates around us. We come up for air and the world crashes back in. My heart is hammering against my ribs as I lean my forehead against hers. Each breath shudders between us.

I move my head and bury my face in her hair and neck. Her arms tighten around me as I breathe in the smell of her skin and hair, lilac mixed with lavender soap. My lips lightly graze her neck and she shivers, pressing her body even closer. I lightly kiss her neck, moving my lips under her jaw to behind her ear. She moans softly and grips the back of my neck guiding my head to her collar bone.

I lightly nip at her soft skin as I move my mouth back up to hers. Our kisses become fiercer. Her mouth opens and I plunge my tongue in, tasting and exploring her mouth. She moans as I move my hands to her waist and tug at her shirt. I want to run my hands over her, feel the warmth of her skin. I realize we are still standing on the porch before the thought is consumed as my hand touches her bare skin. Goosebumps spread across her back as the cold autumn air caresses her. She shivers and moans into my mouth, her hands tugging at my shirt, frantic and desperate.

I yell in pain as my head is wrenched backward, a large hand grasping my hair. Brit jumps away from me with a sharp cry. I don't need to look to know it's Greg. I am so dead.

"Well, isn't this just sweet," Greg sneers into my ear. "I figured I'd catch you trying bang my girlfriend."

"Greg," Brit pleads. "Please. Don't."

"Shut up, you slut!" He barks. "Didn't take you long to hop into the sack with this piece of shit after he sucker-punched me."

"No! That's not the way it happened and you know it!" she argues.

"I told you to shut up!" He yells in my ear.

My hands vainly try to pry his fingers from my hair. I'd have better luck trying to bend steel. I can't see anything but sky and trees.

"What do you want, Greg?" I ask in as a calm a voice as I can. I hope he doesn't notice the tremor in my voice. Hard to sound tough when your head is bent backward and your hair is being pulled out in large clumps.

Greg is silent for a moment. I may have confused him.

"You wanna kick my ass?" I ask. "Fine. Do what you have to. Just leave her out of it."

"Oh don't worry, I've got plans for you," he growls in my ear.

He kicks my legs out from under me. My knees slam into the ground with a bone-jarring crunch. Greg lets go of my hair long enough to back hand me in the side of my head. The world explodes into stars and I tumble to the ground, dazed. It's not the worst hit I've taken. He's big, but my dad has a rage that Greg couldn't even begin to match.

Brit stands defiantly before Greg, trembling with fear. I try to move, but my arms and legs don't want to function. He advances on her. I can tell she's fighting to stand and not bolt back inside the safety of her house. I try to tell her to run, but my voice comes out in a croak. Blood fills my mouth from a split lip. My whole face feels like it has swollen to the size of a grapefruit.

Greg spies the shirt in her hand.

"Oh look!" he cries in triumph as he spies my shirt on the table by her front door. "Did your pansy new boyfriend get you a present?" he mocks, snatching it before Brit can move.

She shakes her head. "No." Her voice is quiet and meek.

Her eyes flick over to me, but I'm still trying to figure out how my limbs work.

Greg lifts my shirt up in front of his face and sneers at it. Somehow I manage to get my feet under me, but my head still feels like it's attached to someone else's body. His shoulders bunch as he slowly pulls his hands further apart. The fabric strains under the pressure. Brit's face is a mask of horror. She's so scared, she can't even move.

With a grunt, he pulls even harder and Brit cries out as the shirt rips. The sound of the tearing fabric is impossibly loud in the still autumn afternoon. She slumps to the ground as Greg throws the tattered remains of my favorite shirt in her face.

I manage a few wobbly steps in her general direction. At the moment, I don't give a damn about Greg. I just need to get between him and her. I can't beat him, but I can keep him from hurting Brit. She doesn't deserve this kind of treatment. Maybe if

I had taken the hits instead of Lela, things would have been different.

Her sneers down at her. "On your knees, Bitch. Just where you belong."

I manage to step between them, spreading my arms and bracing myself against the doorway. Brit sobs behind me. It might look heroic, but the door frame is the only thing keeping me from face planting.

"That's enough, Greg," I slur. My swollen lip makes speaking difficult. The cobwebs are clearing from my head, but I'm still thinking through molasses.

His eyes bulge. I think he's surprised I'm still standing. Hell, I'm surprised I'm still standing. A stiff breeze could blow me over, but he doesn't know that. At least, I hope he doesn't. The important thing is his anger is now focused on me and not Brit. I can't stop my Monster, but I can stop hers.

"I'll say when it's enough! Now move before I beat your ass some more!"

"No." It's a simple word, yet holds so much power. If I wasn't so scared, I'd enjoy the feeling. As it is, my heart is pounding so hard, I'm sure they both can hear it. My legs threaten to buckle and it takes all my flagging strength to keep upright.

Greg's fist slams into the side of my head with enough force that I smack into the door jamb before slumping to the ground in a pile. The world goes black for a moment. When I come to, Greg's truck is squealing off and Brit's crying over me. Pleading with me to say something.

I manage to move my hand up to her head. She clutches my fingers and presses her lips to my palm. My left eye is completely swollen shut. I let out a groan as I pull myself into a sitting position. Brit helps position me against the door before dashing off to get some ice. Brit returns and presses the pack to my face. Cold knifes through the face, tripling the pain. I feel like a pansy when a groan escapes, but I can't stop it.

We're sitting like that when the distinctive crunch of tires on gravel heralds the return of the Thompsons. Specifically, one

Mrs. Thompson, former nurse turned homemaker. Matriarch and unstoppable force of nature. For some reason, she has a soft spot for me. Always has. I've been able to brush off the occasional bump or bruise as being a normal, active boy, but with my face the size of a melon, I doubt she'll listen to anything I say. I can't tell her about Greg because then I would have to explain everything else. But if I don't tell her, then she'll assume it's my dad. Which means she'll call the cops and that will open a whole 'nother can of worms that I really don't want to mess with.

So, I run.

CHAPTER EIGHTEEN

You would think in a small town like Wellsville, the chances of getting lost are slim to none. Apparently, my luck blows. Despite living here my whole life, I have no idea where I am. None of the streets look familiar. Not for the first time, I shoulder the burden of failure. My panicked run from Brit's house led me off into who knows where. To quote the famous animated rabbit, I should have made a left turn at Albuquerque.

It's a good thing my phone has at least a quasi GPS. I shiver at the cold October air. It was warm when I walked to Brits, but now that the sun is setting, I'm regretting my life choices for clothing. I love my jacket, but it's not the warmest thing I own. The glow from the screen bathes everything in an electric light as I wait for it load the maps.

I start hopping to keep warm as my phone struggles to find a signal. It's a serious piece of shit, but it's all I've got at the moment. Finally, it zooms into my location at a blazing one frame per second. I keep expecting it to burst into flames at any moment, but somehow it doesn't. My heart sinks when I see just how far it is to walk home.

There's only one person I can call. My dad. He's going to be pissed, if he's sober. If he's not I'll get to add a few more bruises. Despite the fear gnawing at me, I dial home. The phone rings and rings and rings. I'm about to give up when he answers.

"What the fuck do you want?" He barks into the phone, his

words slurred and almost unintelligible.

"Dad?"

"Where the hell are you?" His volume increases and I start to shake. "You shoulda been home hours ago!" I pretend the tremors and the racing heart are all because of the cold.

"Dad," I say, trying to keep my voice steady. It's a futile gesture, but I try anyway. "I was hoping to get a ride..."

"Don't 'Dad" me, you shit!" He yells, his voice is thick from alcohol, his words smearing together. "If you hadn't been such an asshole to Miranda, she would have stuck around. But no, you had to flaunt that little piece of ass around the house."

Nothing he's saying makes sense, but it still hits me like a punch to the gut.

"Dad, please. It's cold."

He parrots the words but in high pitched voice. "Too fucking bad, asshole!" And with that, the line goes dead.

Adrenaline pushes through my system, fast and hot. I fumble with the phone as I try and shove it in my pocket. It would be just my luck if I dropped the damn thing and it broke. Then I'd really be screwed. Well, more screwed than I am anyway. I know where I am, but it's a long way from where I need to be. I punch a tree in frustration and am rewarded for my stupidity when it fights back. I nurse my torn and bleeding knuckles as tears push against my eyes. It's almost too much to push back, but somehow I do.

If I had any money I could crash at a motel. Going home is out of the question. My dad's in full on Monster mode and I don't need bruises on top of bruises at this point. I can't go back to Blake's. Too many questions, not to mention Brit. I shouldn't have kissed her. If I hadn't been so stupid, none of this would have happened.

So now I'm stuck with nowhere to go and I'm slowly freezing to death. Just great. The universe can just kiss my ass. My phone buzzes with another incoming text. Maybe it's Brit looking for me. I stifle a groan as I see who it's from. Lela. Then it dawns on me that this could be a solution. Maybe I can get her to help me with a room at a motel or something for a couple days. My stomach clenches a little, but I push it away. I can say no.

Lela: Hey.

Me: Hey.

Lela: YA! I've missed you! I've been so worried. <3

Me: I need help.

Lela: *worried* Where are you?

Me: I'm fine. Just need a place to stay for a couple days.

Lela: Of course, baby. :-*

This is a bad idea. I know it is, but sleeping in the park is a worse idea. At least wherever I end up, it'll be warmer than a bench. Besides, after all that has happened, I still miss her. Even if it's mixed up with all sorts of crazy things, she cares. Which is more than I can say for the people who are supposed to be my parents. One's a raging drunk and the other one hasn't bothered to contact me in sixteen years.

I text her my location and try to quell the anxiety over my decision. Nobody else gives a damn, why should I. Besides, if this is a mistake, it won't be my last.

Lela: OMW.

A few cars pass as I wait. Each one slowing as their headlights wash over me. It's enough to get my hopes up but none of them stop once they see my jacket. Even in the dim light it stands out as bad. By the time Lela pulls up next to me, I'm half frozen. I shuffle over to the car and get in. Warmth envelopes me and I groan.

The light blazes on inside the car and Lela lets out a small cry. "Oh baby, what happened?" He hands are gentle as she probes my face. "Oh my god, Jules. I'm so sorry. I should have made you come with me." She starts crying and it wrenches a hole in my heart.

"It wasn't him," I tell her as I wrap my frozen fingers around her trembling hands. "It was some d-bag from school. Promise. I just..." I pause.

"Miss me?" The smile she gives is hopeful, her eyes glittering with emotion.

I nod. "That and my dad is drunk and I just can't deal with any of it right now." I lean my head back and stare at the roof of the car. "I just need a place to stay for a couple days..."

Her smile widens and she squeezes my thigh. I clamp down on the swirl of mixed up feelings threatening to consume me. It's one of the reasons I haven't returned her tweets before now. I'm dancing with fire, but maybe this time I can hold my ground. Is it so wrong to want to be needed by someone?

"Just like a motel or something. I can pay you back when I get paid next."

Her lips purse and she stares of in thought. "Ok. Hotel it is. And if you even try to give me money, I will smack you." Her teasing smile falters at the look on my face. "I'm sorry," she says cupping my cheek. "Poor choice of words."

Shrugging, I blow it off. It wasn't serious. Besides, there are worse things she could do that don't involve hitting. Frying pan and fire. Not sure which is worse, but for the moment? I'll take whatever doesn't involve having my dad use my face as a punching bag. And as warped as our relationship is, Lela at least cares. Which is more than I can say about anyone else in my life right now.

It doesn't take long to find a motel. There's always at least one just off the highway that passes near town. I won't be able to walk, but it's a place to crash and cheap to boot so I won't have to feel bad about taking Lela's money. The less I owe her the less chance that I'll be able to be guilted into doing something I may regret later. What am I thinking, my whole life is regret, guilt, and shame. I said no last time and got the shit beat out of me. Maybe if I had said yes, things would have been different.

"Earth to Jules," Lela says with a light brush of my shoulder. "You can talk to me, babe. You know that. Right?"

If only. I don't say it, but I think it. Honestly, if I knew what was really going on in my head, I'd probably jump off a bridge. "Just...rough day."

She puts a comforting arm around my waist as we climb the

stairs to the room. At least we're inside. The rain drums on the windows muting all other sound and wrapping us in a muffled blanket. Her body is warm against me and I can't stop the shiver that starts at my toes. She pulls me tighter as my teeth chatter from the cold and the maelstrom of feelings in my head.

The door looms, red and peeling. Why do all cheap motels have the same look? Doesn't matter the branding, they all have the same worn out feeling like even they are tired of living and are just going through the motions. But like me, they don't have the guts to end it. Lela draws me into the room. I should resist, but I'm tired. Tired of being. Tired of pain. Tired of hating. I just want something good in my life. Something beyond this hell. But I'm not good enough for a better life.

Casually throwing her keys and purse on a table, she starts tugging at my clothes. "First things first, we need to get you out of these wet clothes."

The fire it ignites inside of me is as nauseating as it is beautiful as each piece of my armor falls to the floor.

She leaves me standing there, dripping, before returning with one of the hotel robes. It scratches my bare skin, but it's dry.

Cupping my cheek, her eyes well up. "You were always so beautiful."

My heart cracks and all of my emotions bleed out. I don't want it to happen, but it's what she does to me. She tears me open and crawls inside, filling each part of me with her. I'm not good enough to make it stop and for once I don't want it to. Maybe that's part of the problem. I've been fighting something I shouldn't. All of this muck inside and I can't even tell what's real or just make-believe. A want to be loved. A need to not have to take care of everything, least of all me.

And that's what she does. My brain checks out and the next moment, she's wiping away tears and cleaning the cuts on my face under the harsh light of the bathroom. Concern is etched across her skin, crinkling her eyes. She's so focused, she has her tongue stuck in a gap of her teeth. It's cute and absurd, and a bubble of laughter pushes up from the depths before spewing forth. There's an edge of hysteria to it, but I don't care. It buoys me up and before long her worried look dissolves into a smile that lights up my world. Reaching up, I stroke her face, so familiar. Yet different because this time, she isn't marred by my father's brutality. Why did I fight this?

Her lips crash into mine and blast the world into a million shining points. And as with so many countless times before, I don't stop her.

CHAPTER NINETEEN

The moonlight crawls through a gap in the blinds and illuminates the faded carpet. Everything is gray. Lela' arm is draped over me and her face is nuzzled into my neck. Her warm, steady breath tickles my skin. Sleep has left me alone with her and I'm terrified. Panic builds inside of me and I want nothing more than to run. Sensing my distress, she instinctively pulls me closer, murmuring into my skin before her voice dissolves into the steady breath of sleep. Her body pressed against mine in that haphazard way that only exists between two lovers.

Images from earlier in the night, before sleep dragged me down, pluck at my mind. Shame fills me as it always does. I allowed her to use me, but at the same time I was using her. She offered me comfort, a place without judgment. Despite my earlier rejections, she never gave up on me. Is this what love means? Two broken people using each other for the things they can't get anywhere else? I want to believe it is, but life isn't like that. What we have isn't love. It's a need to run away. To hide. To escape the pain of life. People like us don't deserve to be loved by normal people. I'm not good enough, I know. It twists my gut to realize that I'm not even good enough for Lela.

Not for the first time, I wonder what life would be like if I just stayed with her. I doubt my dad would try to come looking for me. Maybe he would. We could move to another town. Start up there where nobody knew that I was only seventeen and she was almost thirty. We could pretend we were not the shattered remnants of existence that have so defined us up until that moment. New lives. I let the thought roll through my head, pushing through detritus of my life up until that moment.

Foolish thoughts, I know. Those kinds of things don't happen in real life. Besides, someone would catch on. The bored guy manning the counter at the motel didn't even look at me, but that doesn't mean it couldn't happen. The need to escape everything builds. Escape this town. Escape my father. And with the startling clarity of a sleepless night, I realize I also need to escape Lela. But no matter what I do, I always circle back. I'm tethered to the people who claim to love me yet still find ways to use me. My mind's made up. First thing in the morning, I'll have Lela take me home. I'll grab what I can and I'll leave. I don't know where I'll go. Hell, I don't even have enough money to get further than the next town over. If I'm lucky.

I've never watched her sleep. She always left so that my father wouldn't notice her absence. There were times I wanted her to stay, begged even, desperate for my own comfort. At the time I knew why, but the abandonment felt the same no matter how many times I told myself it was for the best. That she was wrong to do what she was doing. The shame that coated my skin and leeched into my bones. But I'm mesmerized either way. I can't help it. I'm a slave to her and as much as I want to, I can't hate her for it. The person I hate is myself. I could have said no, but the only time I did, turned out to be the biggest mistake of my life so far.

She lets out a quiet moan, her limbs twitching, as she falls deeper into whatever dream she's having. Her breath quickens and her heart pounds against my skin. No, this isn't a dream. This is a nightmare. Something I'm all too familiar with. The fear. The helplessness as monsters born of the deepest part of my psyche tear into my mind. Her moans turn to cries of terror. She beats at against my chest in a desperate attempt to fight off whatever monster has her in its grip. It's all I can do to hold on and whisper soothing words as she fights to be free of her mental prison.

With a violent jerk, she sits up, trembling before dissolving into gasping sobs. I've seen her after my father has raged, and it's nothing compared to the despair I'm witnessing. It breaks my heart and I gather her into my arms as she releases the nightmare's grief.

"Please," she sobs against my chest.

Stroking her hair, I try to soothe away the pain.

Another wrenching cry. "Please don't leave me." Her fingers dig into my arms and I know in that instant, I can't leave her.

"Hush," I whisper. "I won't. I promise." The words burn like acid in my mouth, but I say them anyway. If I had to choose between two monsters, I could do worse than Lela.

Slowly she quiets, but stays cradled in my arms, protected from whatever demons have lurked in her mind. Without a doubt, it's my father. She lived with us long enough to make the scars permanent. Maybe that's why we're drawn together. Shared scars. Shared pain.

"I'm sorry if I scared you," she murmurs into my chest.

My hand continues its journey from the top of her head, to her shoulders and onto her back where the silken strands end before returning to the beginning. She shivers. I lie to myself and pretend that it's from the coating of sweat rather than my hands.

"You didn't scare me." Another pass. Another shiver. I should stop, but I don't want to and it's calming her down which is really the important thing. She needs me, probably more than I need her.

Burrowing deeper into my arms, she murmurs, "Thank you."

I chuckle lightly. "You don't need to thank me for anything. I know how it is to be alone in the dark with echoes of fear ringing in your head."

"I didn't mean that, although I am so glad you were here." She draws back and looks me in the eye, the moonlight dancing across her face. "I mean thank you for not leaving. For wanting to stay with me." Her eyes drop and trace the scar on my collarbone courtesy of my father's rage. "I know..." she halts before raising her eyes to me again. "I know it's been hard and I am so sorry." Her lips brush mine and send fire through my veins. "I love you, Julius."

My heart stops and I don't know what to say. Fear. Guilt. Shame. Wrong. She grips the side of my face and I let out terrified squeak.

"Stay with me, babe," she says stroking my cheeks with her thumbs. "I know it's sudden, but I needed to say it." Her words pick up steam, barreling through me like a train.

I can't breathe. The world darkens as panic sets in. Part of me has wanted this, haven't I? Some dark part wanted to be loved and she's giving it to me and all I can do is freak.

"I needed you to know. That's why I wanted you to come with me. I was scared myself. That's why I acted like I did. Please forgive me, Julius." Tears stream down her face and it does nothing to mar her beauty. Even though I know this is wrong, I can't abandon her. And with that realization, my mind is made up.

Resting my forehead against hers, I say the words that scare me the most yet need to be said. "Run with me." Her eyes widen and I push forward. My heart is pounding, but I won't back down. "Let's run far away from here. Someplace nobody knows who we are and where we can be safe."

Smiling she strokes my face.

"I have some money hidden at my house. We can take that, I can pack some clothes and we can just go. Just you and me."

Pulling my face to hears, she presses her lips hard against mine and I let her. She needs this. She needs me. A yawning pit of guilt opens inside of me and I slam it shut. I'm tired of fighting this. Tired of hating myself for something that may be a horrible idea, but really, I could get used to this. Maybe without my father tearing us both to pieces, we can finally have a real relationship. One where I won't freak out every time she looks at me.

Doubt creeps in the more I sit there with her. This is wrong. I shouldn't be doing this. Blake and his family will be worried. My dad will go ballistic. Especially if he finds out. He'll find us. He'll kill me. With doubt comes the panic again and it's all I can do to keep from screaming. But Lela does notice. Something inside me breaks as she continues kissing me. I don't know what it is, but I feel the void it leaves behind.

I want her to stop, but my struggling only encourages her. I want to talk and plan. She just wants me. In the end, I'll let her because that's what she needs. What I want, isn't important. At least not now. Later we can talk about it. In the morning when she isn't trying to chase away the nightmare with what I can give her. Love. Acceptance. Understanding. The physical part is the only way I can show it to her. Words aren't real. Actions are.

Uncurling from my lap, she presses me into the bed and straddles me before raining hard kisses down upon my mouth, face, and neck. Each touch of her mouth is agony against the bruises left by Greg's fists. It sparks something primal inside of me when she drags her teeth across my collarbone. I'm helpless under her assault, but I push away the fear and pull away into that dark place I hide in when she's like this. My body can do what she wants while the rest of me curls inside, immune to the shame and guilt. It's a quiet place where I don't have to think about anything. Nothing can touch me here. The walls will tremble, especially with Lela, but they never fall.

Tears course down my cheeks, but I don't feel the sadness behind them. She's hurting me, but I don't feel it. I'm floating in the void between emotions. Besides, I know she doesn't hurt me because she hates me. My father and Greg already take that place. It's just what happens when she loses herself in her own pain and is desperate to be free. Besides, she loves me, and I want to make her happy. She's had enough pain in her life without me making it worse. What she does to me is nothing compared to what others have done. People like my father. I'm sure there were others before him. There would have to be for the way she is.

The walls shudder and I want to break out and hold her again. Take her pain and fear away so she doesn't have to hurt anymore. That must be what the tears are for. Not the physical pain, the dark guilt of those first nights she came to me. I was confused back then. I didn't know what she wanted until she showed me. No, I'm crying because I can't fix her.

CHAPTER TWENTY

"You don't have to do this, honey," Lela says probably for the fortieth time since we got up.

I respond the same way I have the previous thirty-nine times. "Yes, I do. The money I have stashed isn't a lot, but it'll be enough to cover some of our expense."

She's calmer than last night, but there is a tension in her hands and face. Prying one of her hands off the wheel, I pull it over to me. Slight tremors work from her fingers into me. She's scared. Maybe more than I am. I know it's wrong to ask her to do this. I've fought with my brain since early this morning.

"It'll be ok," I say as I work the tension from hand. "He was pretty hammered last night. I don't expect he'll wake up before noon and by then, we'll be long gone."

Gulping, she nods and gives my hand a slight squeeze. "You're a beautiful soul, Julius." She gives me a slight smile. "Besides, you flash those doe eyes of yours and I can't say no."

Her tone is light, but the tension is still lingering in the corners of her mouth. My phone buzzes before I can respond. Probably a good thing as I'm the one who can't say no to her, even when I've tried. Anger flares as Blake's face lights up on my screen. I shouldn't be mad at him but it's still there. I needed him and he ditched me for someone else. Maybe I'm just too needy. Maybe he's tired of dealing with my shit. I know I am.

Blake: Hey

Me: Hey.

Blake: Marcus said you called last night.

Me: Yeah…

Blake: You ok?

Me: Yeah. I'm fine. Thx for asking.

Blake: Brit told me about Greg.

Me: Which part? The part where she was dating him or the part where he bounced my face off your door jam?

Blake: …both. I wish you would have told me.

Me: I did. I told you he was being a douche.

Blake: I mean about Brit.

Ice floods through me. Does he know about me kissing Brit? Did she tell him. My hand shakes a little as I type my response. Better to not discuss it. If she hasn't told him. Then it'll be really awkward. Besides, it's not his damn business anyway.

Me: She's your sister. Ask her.

He doesn't respond for a long time. Lela squeezes my thigh. I was so intent on the screen, I didn't even notice. Now I see that her hand has been slowly working its way up my leg. The phone vibrates and I let a slight yelp. Lela quickly removes her hand and grips the steering wheel, her knuckles white. A hurt look passes over her face. Shame wells up. I didn't mean to upset her.

"Hey," I brush her shoulder with my fingertips, and she shudders at the contact. "I didn't mind." I wish I didn't mind, but it's not about me. "I was just…" I hold up the phone.

Taking my hand she rests it on her leg. It should be an innocent touch, but nothing ever is with Lela. She moves her leg side to side so that I'm rubbing her thigh without moving my hand. Inside I want to scream, but I'm not sure entirely why. Lela still feels wrong no matter how much time I spend with her. It shouldn't. I should be enjoying that a beautiful woman wants me. But it doesn't stop the burning inside as she repositions my hand higher.

I force my mind to focus on the screen and not what Lela is doing.

Blake: We need to talk.

Me: Ok. Talk.

Blake: Not like this, man.

Me: Well, I'm busy right now.

Blake: Later?

Me: Maybe.

It's like I've forgiven him but not really. Still, my frustration builds; and I stab the power button until the phone turns off, so he can't call me.

"You ok, honey?" Lela asks.

Sighing, I shove my phone in my pocket, grateful that it requires my left hand. The pout she gives me when I'm not touching her is almost funny, but I'm not in the mood to give into it.

"Yeah. Just…Blake being Blake."

"Blake is a good friend," she says, her smile wistful. I wonder what—or who—she's lost.

Do monster's regret? My father used to when my mom left. I'd wake up to him crying and staring at her picture. I knew he'd moved on when he threw it against the wall. His picture of her. His regret broken in that moment. I carefully picked the broken shards of glass and stole it. Hid the photo away where he couldn't hurt her anymore. Does Lela have a shattered photo? It hurts to even think about it. Hurts in a way that tears holes inside that bleed sorrow into the void.

"What do you mean?" My voice comes out a little rougher than I intend and her eyes widen a little.

Fear is etched across her face and I hate myself. "I mean that he's always been a good friend to you. I mean, you've told me so much about him." Her voice trembles a little. "I mean, I've never met him, but he sounds like a great guy…" As her words trail off, tears well in her eyes. Not for the first time, the real fear I could turn into a monster rears its ugly head.

"I'm…sorry." I want to defend myself but trying would just make it worse. That's what my father would do. Every time he'd hurt her, he would always apologize and beg forgiveness. But it wouldn't stop him next time. It was a vicious cycle of crap and I didn't want to repeat that. Not with her. Not with anyone.

"I don't want to be a monster..." The words fall out of my mouth before I realize what I've done.

The tires screech as she slams on the brakes. The seatbelt locks and she swings us off to the side of the road. My heart pounds so fast I worry it will explode. I look over and Lela's eyes are a mixture of pain and anger.

Grabbing my face me she bores holes through me. "Don't. Ever. Say. That." Her words are clipped and she's panting.

I try to shrink away, but her hand is a vise. Fear consumes me and I let out a small whimper. Her eyes soften at the sound and her hand relaxes to cup my cheek.

Tears still course down her face, but the anger is gone from her eyes. "Julius." She pauses to lean over and rest her forehead against mine. Her fingers and hands roam across my face and hair. "Oh Julius. You will never be him. You're too kind." She kisses me, her lips soft against mine. "Besides, I won't let you."

"But..." She silences my words with her mouth. I am her prisoner, and a part of me couldn't be happier. The rest of me wants to run. But running from Lela has gotten me nowhere. Besides, if I'm with her, she won't be lonely anymore and maybe I won't either. We'll make it work. For the second time in two days, I kiss her back with the same intensity that she has. I tell myself I want this. She needs this from me. One of these days I'll be able to feel the same for her.

A horn honks followed by a whoop and everything snaps back in focus. We're on the side of the road and my hand is halfway under her shirt. With a frustrated growl she pulls away. Her eyes are bright and I know I've done the right thing. She's happier than she has been in so long. It makes me feel good. Another honk. Another holler and she smiles wickedly at me. I try and hide inside my jacket. I can feel the blush spreading across my face. With a laugh more carefree than I've ever heard from her, she puts the car in gear and swings back out onto the road.

"I love how you get me," Lela says after a moment.

Warmth spreads through me and I smile a real smile. Not the

fake ones that I've been using to keep people from asking what was wrong, but a real one. The kind that makes you feel like you can do anything and maybe the world isn't a giant hole of suck. It was only a moment before reality snuffed it out, but hope remained. Maybe, just maybe, things would work out the way I wanted instead of the universe's sick joke. Deep down, I know it'll crash and burn, but I can't think of that now. One foot in front of the other. If I stop, I'll die. If I look back, I'll stumble.

Lela is more relaxed now. Instead of panicked glances, she flashes me a warm smile. It melts my insides and helps banish the icy fear I usually feel when I'm with her. Honestly, I'm not even sure what I've been so scared of. Yes, she gets a little rough sometimes, and there's the whole awkwardness of us being so far apart in age, but why should this be a bad thing. I deserve to be happy. She deserves to be happy. For the first time, I actually don't care what anybody else—my father, Blake, anyone—thinks about this. I don't know if it's love or just two people finding some comfort in this life. Whatever it is, I can't let something stupid like fear get in my way.

So when Lela pulls up in front of my house, I feel invincible. I'm out the door before the car even stops moving and then reality hits me like a brick wall. Inside this house is my father, the monster. Lurking in the shadows. The world shifts and I'm five again. My father's hands reaching from the dark to clamp around my mother's neck, her cries cut short as the air is crushed from her throat. Fear steals my own air as I sit there hopeless, watching. She thrashes against him leaving long bloody rents in arms. He smiles, spittle oozing from lips stretched into a manic grin. But she doesn't stop fighting. Raising a massive hand he smashes it into her face. The moment is thick with fear and blood. I can taste it in my mouth as it covers her skin and clothes. My heart lurches in my chest and I remember being scared she was dead. Her eyes. I can't see her face but her eyes, dark as the night sky, find mine behind swollen lids. She tries to offer comfort, but I can't see them anymore. I just see the muscles in his arms as he tears her clothes with his thick fingers. I want to scream, but I know what will happen if I do.

A voice drifts through the void. I think it's my mom, but it can't be. She left shortly after that night. Abandoned me because I couldn't save her. No, this voice is Lela. The memory cracks. Time. Now. I'm outside my father's house, the memory of that night like a raw wound on my soul but Lela is here. Her arms protect me as I sob into her shoulder.

"Come on, Jules," she whispers while rubbing circles in my back. "Let's get out of here. We don't have to do this."

Pulling back, I scrub my face and force the memory back into it's tiny box full of childish fear and a pounding heart. The sweaty moments hidden in the closet pretending I was invisible, so he wouldn't find me.

"No," I say, hating the quiver of fear in my voice. "I have to do this. I worked too hard to save up this money. If I leave it, he'll just spend it all on booze."

She searches my eyes a moment before nodding. "Ok," she says taking a calming breath. "Besides, if we're quiet he shouldn't wake up. Right?"

Hiding my fear behind a fake smile, I force my legs to not run the other way. Each step across the broken concrete makes me cringe as it crunches beneath my feet. Lela's steps are quieter. The sound fills me with the unreasonable, but gripping, fear that any noise could wake my father from his alcohol induced slumber. It's a risk coming here, but I can't back down. I won't let him take anything else from me. He already took my mom.

Lela's hand finds mine and gives it a comforting squeeze. Lacing our fingers together, I take a steadying breath and ease the front door open.

CHAPTER TWENTY-ONE

The place is trashed even worse than normal. Empty beer cans are scattered about the room with a large, half-empty bottle of liquor so cheap it might as well be paint thinner sitting square on the coffee table. The room reeks of alcohol and vomit. I glance at Lela and see a combination of disgust and fear. Her fingers tighten and I can feel her whole body tremble as she presses close. Not for the first time I question the sanity of this whole situation.

Side by side we navigate through the wasteland of garbage to the stairs, careful not to step on anything. I've only been gone a day. It's hard to believe he did all this, but really, I shouldn't be surprised. I could tell when he answered the phone that he was hitting the bottle hard. We're almost to the stairs when Lela trips over an errant can and stumbles into the wall with a loud thump. We both freeze, waiting for the telltale sounds of someone moving upstairs. When we don't hear anything, I motion her to follow.

No matter how hard I try, there is always one step that creaks loud enough to wake the dead. Our bodies tense to run, ears straining for the noise of my father waking up. If it wasn't so serious, I'd probably fall over laughing. As it is, hysterical laughter builds up inside of me, twisting my face into a lunatic grin. The more I think about it, the worse it gets. Lela lets out a very muffled snort and it's all we can do to hurry into my room and bury our faces into pillows before the laughter takes hold.

As quick as it hits, the feeling disappears and I'm left with aching sides, and a hollow feeling in my chest. Lela squeezes my hand when I stand up and quietly close my door. I don't have much, but spare clothes will be a necessity. There's still blood on my shirt from where Greg hit me yesterday. Stripping it off, I grab a clean shirt and stuff some more into a duffel bag. Blake gave it to me once when he was trying to get me to work out with him. I tried it a couple times, but never could stick with it like he does. Still, the bag comes in handy when I need to spend time away from home.

The money I've stashed in a small box taped to the bottom of my dresser. I toss it with my clothes in the duffel and pass it off to Lela. If I'm leaving, I'm bringing my sewing kit with me. I do my best to be quiet as I slide it out from under the bed. Still it makes the occasional scraping noise that sets us both on edge. Lela keeps looking at her watch and I know we've been here too long. I've just about managed to get it free when I hear the noise I've been dreading. My father's awake. Fear closes my throat, the toilet flushes, and I heave on the wooden box, uncaring of the noise it makes. Speed is required now.

Lela is the first out of the door. I pause to take a quick glance around for the last time. I won't ever be back. Stepping into the hall, I'm there just in time to see my father's fist connect with Lela's jaw. Her body goes limp and tumbles down the stairs. I let out a wordless cry before he turns his baleful gaze towards me. There is no love in those eyes. Only hatred.

"Well lookie who's home," my dad slurs, a bottle clutched in one hand. "I was wondering where you'd run off to." His eyes flick down the stairs to where Lela is.

I can't see her, but I hear a stifled moan so I know she isn't dead. I want to move, but I don't know where. He's between me and Lela. There is no escape.

"I know what you've been doing, you little bastard," he says. "You were banging her behind my back. Getting your old man's sloppy seconds."

I clamp my mouth shut as the anger and shame start mixing

inside me.

"No wonder she left. Just like your bitch of a mother." He's taken a few more steps and the stench of alcohol fills my nose. "They loved you, more than me."

He's not yelling which makes this all the more terrifying. If it were pure rage, I could handle it. But this? This is cold, calculated, deadly. I'm like a deer in the headlights as he takes first one step, then another, and another. The distance between us shrinking and I can't move, frozen between fear and indecision, until he is standing within arms' reach of me. His body is tense, coiled, like a spring, ready to strike at a moment's notice. I can see each vein and muscle in his arms, a roadmap of violence ending with the bottle clutched in his white knuckled hand. When it moves, it's without warning. At his side one second and the next it is screaming towards my face.

Reflexes born of years living with this monster kick in and the bottle misses my head, the brown glass catching my hair before exploding in a shower of razor shards and beer. It peppers my face and hands. Each sliver a burning spike across my skin. My father lets out a roar of anger as he too is caught in the back blast. Blinded, I stumble into my room. My only exit, my window, stands between me and a long drop to the ground. I don't have time to think, I just move. If I stop to close my door, he'll catch me. Right now, he's yelling and punching the wall. I'm guessing he ended up with glass in his eye. Either way, I use my sewing box as a battering ram. The window is no match for the military constructed box and it bursts through without effort. I follow after it heedless of the glass tearing at my clothes and skin. The small slope of roof gives me a moment of solid before I'm tumbling into space, the ground rushing toward me.

Despite the adrenaline screaming through me, the impact shatters my senses. My rib cage compresses as my body absorbs the shock. My father's incoherent rage echoes from my window. The sound is hollow, muted, as I struggle to pull my brain back into motion. I don't have time to focus on injuries as my meager possessions start raining down on me. A shirt, a poster, a rock I found while walking one day. These bits of my life are discarded in a vain attempt to further injure me. Stumbling, I lurch away from the house, taking only a moment to gather my sewing box. Somehow it survived the fall in one piece. I stagger towards the back fence as my father continues to expend his rage on what remains of my room.

Neighbors peak out from behind drawn curtains, but nobody says anything. Things like this are not an uncommon occurrence in this neighborhood. People mind their own business. My last barrier to freedom is a six foot, rotting wood fence. I pray that my box survives another fall as I pitch it up and over. My body screams in protest as I drag myself over the fence to the alleyway. I'm still in survival mode and I scoop up my one remaining possession before turning and running as fast as my bruised and cut body will go. There is no going back. He won't follow me now but if I stop, I won't be able to move again. Panic and shame slam into me at the thought of Lela lying at the bottom of the stairs. I can only hope she was able to recover and get away. Thoughts of what he might do to her if she isn't are more terrifying than I can imagine.

Lungs aching, I collapse in the alley behind a gas station and fish my cell out of my pocket. I consider calling the police, but they wouldn't get there in time. They never have before. My choices for refuges have dwindled to none. So I hit speed dial and pray that Blake answers. After a couple rings, I fear that Marcus is screening my calls, but someone answers just before the call dumps to voicemail.

Sounds of loud talking and even louder music assault my ear.

"Hello," Blake answers.

"Blake?" I wince when my voice cracks. I sound weak and scared and I hate myself for it.

The voices and music fade as he must have stepped outside to talk. Blake at a party. Not his usual M.O., but not the most uncommon thing in the world. He's gotta have other hobbies than dealing with my worthless ass all the time.

"Julius? Are you ok? Marcus said you called but he didn't say why."

At least Marcus said something.

"No. I…uh…need you to pick me up. My dad…" I stop before I let out the truth. I don't want to talk about it on the phone.

The line is silent for a moment. "Where are you?" Blake asks. There's a tone to his voice, I haven't heard before. He's angry. He's never angry.

"Listen, if you're busy, I can…"

Blake sighs, a big whoosh of air. "No," he says more calmly. "Just tell me where. I'll be there."

I tell him where to pick me up and then I huddle in my jacket. Now that the adrenaline has left my system, I'm freezing. I didn't have time to grab a coat. It's unlikely my father will come looking for me, but if he does, I can only hope that Blake gets here first. I try Lela's number but it dumps to voicemail, so her phone must be off. I hope she's ok. I've lost everything else in my life, I don't want to lose her too. Maybe she's hiding too. I can only hope for the best but hoping doesn't stop the swirling dark thoughts. Her face bleeding, unable to move as my father descends on her. I choke back a sob and focus on the now. It doesn't stop the fear, but it's better than curling into a ball.

It's too dark to see the damage, but it feels like there are thousands of cuts on my face and body. Every muscle and bone throbs. Moving is excruciating. I force the pain, both physical and emotional, into a tiny box and put it away. I've got a warehouse of these moments in my head, this one is the worst.

Blake pulls up and screeches to a halt in front of me. The headlights blind me for a moment, putting my life in a stark relief, exposing every flaw and scar. Two car doors open and I wonder who is with him. I hope it isn't Brit. She doesn't need to see me like this.

"Jesus!" Marcus exclaims.

"Julius!" Blake kneels in front of me, grabbing my shoulders. "What the hell happened?"

Worry is etched across his face and I can't help a tear sliding down my cheek.

"He needs a doctor," Marcus saves me from talking. "We can worry about what later."

Blake nods, his eyes burning with anger. I can't help but shrink from their intensity. God, I'm a mess. He pulls back, closes his eyes, and takes a calming breath.

"Can you walk," he asks after a moment.

"Yeah," I croak. "I walked here." I give him a weak smile that turns into a wince as the wounds on my face stretch and crack.

Blake and Marcus help me stand and I limp towards the car, while Marcus retrieves my sewing box.

"What the heck happened to this?" he asks lifting the box up like it was nothing. "Throw it out of a window or something?"

I look over at the battered footlocker. It's scuffed and dirt is embedded in the latch and hinges. It even has a piece of glass stuck to it. I start laughing, a choking wheezing sound. Marcus and Blake give each other a weird look. I know I look like shit, but at the same time I don't care.

CHAPTER TWENTY-TWO

I manage to get my insanity under control by the time we get to the hospital. Getting committed would not be the best thing for me. Besides, Lela wouldn't be able to call me when she gets the chance. Mostly, I just want to be left alone, to withdraw from everything and just hide until it's all over. Not likely now that we're at the hospital. Pretty soon they'll be asking me questions and I won't be able to lie to them. Lying takes too much energy and I'm done. There is nothing left inside but an empty hole. Years of lying and hiding, and I don't even have that anymore. It's all gone.

"Hey Jules," Blake says after the nurses leave. "How are you?"

I shrug. "I've been worse."

I mean it as a joke, but Blake pales a little. Guess my grin was more of a grimace with all tape and super glue holding my face closed.

"I'm joking," I say with a dismissive wave. "Thanks for sticking around."

Blake sits down. The room, more like curtained off area in the ER, is small. It's a false sense of privacy. I can hear everything going on around me from the woman sobbing about an accident, to the kid crying over a broken arm.

"So what did they say?"

I shrug again. "I'll live. Have to be careful as they had to put a couple stitches in."

"Are you going to tell them what happened?"

I turn away. He doesn't know the details, but it doesn't take a rocket scientist to figure out that the cuts on my face aren't from the window considering I smell like a bar. Also, jumping from said window and the associated cuts and bruises.

"Julius," Blake pleads. "You need to tell them."

"Why? What good will it do?" My voice raises as tears threaten. "My dad's an asshole. I get that, but I don't have anywhere else to go."

Blake's face darkens and a muscle jumps in his jaw. He wants to say something, but I barrel on. I've been pushed around too much. It's my life. I can do what I damn well please.

"You don't know what it's like. Besides you weren't there."

It's a low blow, but at the moment, I don't care. He would have picked me up if Marcus hadn't hung up on me. Then I wouldn't have shown up with Lela. My dad wouldn't have guessed that anything had ever happened between the two of us. I should be pissed at Marcus, but he isn't in the room right now. Besides, he's not my friend. Blake is and has always been there no matter what. That is, until Marcus. I can't figure out what's going on there. Marcus is almost acting like a jealous boyfriend, but that can't be right. Blake isn't like that. He would have told me.

"I'm sorry," he says, defeat written across his face.

My anger evaporates and is replaced with the dull, hollow feeling again. I'm too tired to be mad. How a void can be so heavy is beyond me. The weight forces my shoulders down into a hunch. My eyes fall to my hands resting on the blanket. If I was good friend, I would apologize. I don't even know anymore. Somewhere along the way, someone pulled the rug out from beneath me and exposed a giant pit. Like in a cartoon, except not funny.

"Where's Marcus?" I mumble as I stare at my hands, desperate to stop my swirling thoughts.

"Waiting room. I'll probably have to pry the nurses off him before too long," he says with a weak smile.

I manage to snort, which breaks the weight over me. It'll be back. It always is, but for the moment, everything is good. Blake and I are good. A smile breaks across his face and he grips my arm. Maybe I don't need to apologize this time.

"Go save Marcus. I'm not going anywhere," I say, pulling the blanket back to expose the huge bandage covering my shin. I didn't even realize it was bleeding until they started cleaning me up.

Blake gulps and nods his head. Dammit. I shouldn't have shown it to him. I meant it to be funny. Instead I made him feel worse. I grab his hand before he can walk away.

"Hey. I'll be ok."

He doesn't say anything, just nods his head, gives my hand a squeeze and leaves. I lean back and wait. The doctor mentioned that a counselor would be down to talk to me, but I'm on hospital time. It could be forever.

The curtain parts and a brown-haired woman enters. She's not dressed in scrubs, but rather slacks and a simple blouse. Her hair is pulled back from her face and wire-rimmed glasses are perched on her nose. Freckles dot her pale face, highlighted by the faint flush of someone who was in a hurry. She grabs my chart from the end of the bed and glances at it briefly before replacing it.

"Hello, Julius. I'm Felicia. Sorry it took me so long," she says as she sits in the chair next to me. "This hospital is like a maze sometimes."

I give her a confused look. I have no idea who she is or what she is doing here.

She blinks and a slight blush creeps up her neck.

"Oh!" She stammers. "I'm sorry. Since you're still technically a minor, I've been assigned as your social worker."

I grimace. "Great. Listen, I just want to go home. I'm tired and I've been here so long my ass has fallen asleep."

Felicia doesn't even bat an eyelash at my frustration.

"Well, that's what I'm here for," she says, pulling a notepad from her bag. "But first we need to talk about what happened tonight with your father."

"Nothing happened. My father was pissed. I left. End of

story." I give her my best glare but it doesn't even faze her either.

She chews on the end of her pen for a moment in thought. He eyes travel over the cuts on my face. I wait for her judgment. She doesn't believe me. It's clear by the way she's looking at me.

"You don't need to protect him, Julius."

"What?" I ask, my walls firmly in place. "Protect who? I'm not protecting anybody. I told you what happened."

"Julius," she says patiently, her eyes piercing.

The small part of me that I keep hidden trembles. My hands shake and I hug myself to keep them still. I can't let her see my weakness.

"Julius," she says again, quiet and calm. "You're safe now. He can't hurt you anymore, but you need to be honest with me. Please, tell me what happened."

My eyes fill with unbidden tears as my defenses crack. I rub my eye with the heel of my hand, wiping the tears away. I don't want to tell her, but there is a part of me that just wants it to be over. Guilt and shame flood through me.

Felicia folds her hands around one of mine, her fingers cool and soft. Understanding, not judgment, fills her eyes. Maybe I can trust her. I don't know. My brain is so full of stuff, I can't even think straight. But to be free of the Monster. Is that even possible?

"My father…" my voice is halting and quiet.

Felicia nods in encouragement.

"He…he was drinking…" The floodgates open and tears pour down my cheeks as I tell her about the Monster. About the fear, the anger, the lock on my bedroom door. My mouth tries to tell her about Lela but some secrets I need to keep. I clamp my lips shut.

Felicia brushes tears from her eyes and takes a sip from a bottle of water. To my surprise, she doesn't run screaming. She's not scared of me or my father. She just sits there listening and holding my hand, waiting for the torrent of pain to subside. It does eventually, leaving me drained. She lets go of my and sits back, her face thoughtful.

"Now," she says, pulling the pen out of her mouth. "We need

to do a couple things. Ok?"

I nod, my voice is worn out and I'm too tired to talk.

"One, we need to find you a place to stay for the next few days. Two, we need to talk to the police about what has been going on."

I shrink in on myself. The very idea of talking to the police is more than I can take. Felicia seems to notice because she grabs my hand again.

"It's ok, Julius. I can talk to the police tonight and tell them what happened. But you'll need to go talk to them soon if you want to keep him out of your life. Ok?"

"What if I don't want him out of my life? I mean, I don't have anybody else. My mom's gone and now you're asking me to give up my dad?"

Felicia gives my hand a squeeze. "I know, Julius. It'll be ok. I promise. You need a safe place. Somewhere that you don't have to worry about jumping out of a window to escape."

She's right, but I feel so guilty. I wish Lela were here.

She continues. "You need to be someplace where you don't have to be the adult. Understand?"

I manage a weak nod.

"Now, is there a family member you can stay with? An aunt? Uncle? Grandparent?"

"No."

"Ok, well, we need to find you a home with a responsible party, an adult that can be your legal guardian for the time being. I don't have any foster arrangements right now. What about your friend? Does he live with his parents?"

"Blake? Yeah. He does. I've stayed there a few times already."

Felicia nods. "Ok, well I can let you stay there a few days, but we will have to get some more permanent living arrangements made." Felicia pats my hand and pulls a card out of her bag. "This is my card. If you need to talk. Anytime. Just give me a call. I have your cellphone number and I'll get Blake's home number from him." She gives me a warm smile. "We'll work this out. Ok?"

"Thank you," I say slumping back into my pillow. I'm

exhausted and just want to go to bed.

"I'll be in touch. Just so you know, the police may call you regarding your statement. Without it, they can't do anything to protect you. Understand."

"Yeah," I mumble.

Felicia sets her card on my tray before leaving. I pull my thin hospital blanket up to my chin and curl up into a ball. Now for the waiting.

CHAPTER TWENTY-THREE

Talking to the police has always been nerve-wracking. Chalk it up to bad parenting. I mean, every time the cops came to my house, bad things happened after they left. My father hates them and he's passed some of that loathing onto me. Not that they are necessarily bad people, but there is always a fear lurking whenever I'm face to face. I'm on my guard. Deep down I know I'll say something that will get me in trouble. Something like Lela.

Not to mention, I'd rather be at work doing something productive. I owe the Thompson's big and I need to be on my best behavior if I ever want to feel like I'm not a leech.

Officer Romero sits on the other side of the table, a cup of coffee steaming next to her. It doesn't matter who comes to the house, Mrs. Thompson always offers them something to eat or drink. Saying no isn't an option. Not that anyone could resist her easy smile and genuine attitude. Although I'm not sure caffeine is something Romero needs. She is a bundle of energy. Small, yet has an air of confidence that has me trying to huddle into a small ball. Still, like Mrs. T, she has a quick smile that lights up her whole face. However, I can see the anger in her eyes as I recount last night's horror. I don't tell her about Lela. That would have been a whole other list of questions that I don't want to even get into. Besides, they went to the house and nobody was there. No Lela. No dad.

While I wait for her to write her report, I fire off yet another text to Lela. She hasn't responded to any of the other messages I've sent and I'm getting worried.

"Something bothering you, Julius?" Romero asks, her pen poised over the paper.

I hurry to smooth my features and shake my head. By the way her eyes narrow, I can tell she doesn't believe me.

"Julius." Her tone is patient, but there is a warning in there too. "If you don't tell me everything, I can't help you."

My brain kicks into high gear and I scramble to say something to keep her from probing. "My father," I manage to say.

Reaching out she gives my hand a squeeze. "It'll be ok." Her smile is back. "We have an APB out on him. If he shows his face anywhere, we'll get him. You don't have to be scared of him anymore."

But I am scared. Nobody was at the house when the police arrived last night. No dad. No Lela. Now I'm terrified that he'll show up and end what he started last night. That's how it works in my life. I can't get away. He might be gone for now, but he'll be back. I wrap my arms around my stomach as fear chills me. They won't go looking for him. He's not that important and despite Romero's assurances, neither am I. Police can't do anything until a crime has been committed. My guess is that my father will hide out until everything dies down and then saunter back into my life like he always does.

"Now as far as where you can stay." Romero pauses to look me in the eye and my heart sinks.

"I'll get my stuff packed," I manage to get out around the giant lump in my throat.

Quirking an eyebrow at me, her smile gets warmer. "There is no need for that."

She laughs, a rich, heartfelt sound full of life and happiness at the obvious shock on my face.

"Your case manager told me the Thompson's had signed up to be a foster home some time ago." Closing her notebook, she takes a long sip of coffee. "They just need to fill out some paper work, get a home inspection and then you can stay here as long as you want."

Sunlight explodes in my chest and I have to fight to hide the tears threatening to follow them. I don't want to embarrass myself in front of her. She doesn't know me and I don't want to look weak. Besides, I like her despite my earlier misgivings. There is something about her that puts me at ease.

Dipping me head, I say, "Thank you."

Standing up, Romero gives my shoulder a light squeeze as she heads out. "We'll take care of him. You don't have to worry about anything. Leave that up to me."

I nod, not trusting my voice.

"And if he tries anything, call us. I'll be there." As she heads towards the door, she calls out, "Thanks for the coffee, Mrs. T! Tell Blake I said hi."

Mrs. T's voice echoes an affirmative from further in the house.

Slumping I stare at the clock. It's not even lunch and I feel drained. The urge to crawl back into bed is overwhelming, but I promised Mr. T I would help out at the shop today. Now I'm regretting all my decisions. My phone buzzes and I scramble like a madman to dig it out of my pocket. The hope it's from Lela dies when I just see it's a payment reminder. Straw meet camel. As if I didn't have enough to worry about, I have this. Not to mention having to go to my dad's place to grab what few clothes I have to my name. But first, I have to a responsible person. Dark thoughts fill my brain and I grab my coat, stomp outside, and slam the door behind me. It's childish and I hate myself for doing it, but I can't help the boiling anger at the cruel joke my life has become. I should be grateful. I'm sure there's some loser out there with it worse than me. I mean, at least I have a roof over my head. I have a way out, but I'm just fucking fed up with everything. I just want to be left alone. Ignored. But not really. I want a family like Blake's. One that isn't in pieces and missing chunks.

The clouds hang heavy above me full of rain or maybe snow considering how my breath pools in a fog around me as I walk. The wind bites at my skin and the remains of leaves crunch underfoot. I can't wait until spring when I'm not freezing my ass off everywhere. Universe: 4000. Me: -12.

Jamming my hands in my pockets, I hurry towards the welcoming warmth of the shop door. Heat. Blessed heat envelopes me making my skin tingle where the biting wind had scoured it raw. Blake looks up, his eyes expectant until he sees me. It's obvious I'm the last person he wants to see. Not sure what his problem is, but his weird behavior is really pissing me off. And to be honest, I'm a little mad at him too. Maybe a lot mad. If he had answered my call the other night, none of this crap would have happened. I almost mentioned Lela to the cops but I didn't want to have to explain everything. Besides, she's disappeared before. If he had killed her, there would have been a body. I shudder at the possibility.My dad a fugitive. The more I think on it the angrier I get.

"What?" I snap. As soon as the words leave my mouth, I realize I'm itching for a fight...and it feels good.

His eyes darken. "What the hell, Julius?"

"Hey, I wasn't the one giving out nasty looks when I walked in here," I fire back.

He still hasn't moved from his chair, but I can see a muscle twitching in his cheek. "Whatever. I know things have been rough, but you don't have to take out on me."

"Rough?" The word explodes out of me in disbelief.

Of all the people, he has no right to take what I have gone through and package it up in a simple little word. It isn't simple. It's crap.

"Rough?" I repeat again, my voice rising. "What the hell do you know about rough? You have this perfect fucking life where everyone loves you. Nothing bad ever happens to you and at the end of the day, you get to go home to nice home where nobody is trying to fucking bash your head in with a goddamn bottle!"

I've stepped over a line and I don't want to stop. I want him, hell everyone, to feel all this crap inside of me. All the doubt, fear, pain. I want to smash them in the face with it until they can see me. Blake's stares at me open mouthed. In another time, I'd find it funny. Now, it sends me over the edge. Grabbing a chair, I fling it across the room where it bounces off the linoleum before skidding to stop against the wall. I reach for another one, and Blake pins my arms to my sides. I fight against them, but it's like trying to move a mountain. Panic wells up and my attempts to free myself get more frantic. Still he won't let go. My rage turns to blind fear. I won't let him hurt me. The thought galvanizes me and I slam my foot down on his. He lets out a grunt and his grip loosens just enough that I rip free. Blake is big, but I'm faster and I use it to my advantage. I know that I can't really hurt him much but I still put everything I can into the punch. My focus narrows to a point on his chin. Just before I connect, I see his whole face. I see his fear. He knows what's coming. He could stop me, but he doesn't. In that moment, I try to stop, but my momentum is too much. I've committed to the swing.

Blake has always been my strength. My rock. My only friend in this horrible world. Now I'm standing over him, my hand throbbing. I don't remember the actual point of contact. Everything disappeared in a hot flash of emotion. What's left of my world crumbles and I realize it has all been my fault. All of it. His eyes fill with the hurt of my betrayal. Despite what I've done, he doesn't fight back. There is no accusation in his eyes, just pain.

I can't take it anymore and I bolt. I have nowhere to go, but I can't stay here. This is my fault. Opening the door, I come face to face with Marcus, my speed too much for either of us to react in time. The tray of coffee in his hands explodes in a shower of scalding liquid, dousing us both. He lets out a shout of surprise as I bounce off of him and half stumble, half run, into the snow. I hear Blake call out to me. I don't deserve him. I don't deserve anyone. I pick up the pace and dodge between houses. He could outrun me, but he doesn't. I don't look back, I just barrel on into the snow leaving the last piece of my life behind me. The Thompson's won't want me anymore. Not after what I did. Hell, Marcus will probably arrest me on site.

The snow muffles my footsteps and the cold freezes the tears to my face. The air sears my lungs and saps my strength. Before long I'm walking. I don't have the strength or will to keep moving. Cars pass, but nobody slows. No sirens to herald the police coming for me. It's almost dark when I get to the only place I have ever called home. It's not really home, but it's all I deserve. At least my father isn't here. He can't see me like this and in a few minutes, I won't have to worry about anything ever again. The thought should scare me, but it doesn't. It's a relief. No more pain. No more fear. No more monsters hiding inside the people I love.

With purpose comes strength and I walk up the snowy steps for the last time.

CHAPTER TWENTY-FOUR

Fitting that the last things I see are the broken remains of my house. It was always a war zone but the wreckage this time is post-apocalyptic. I can only hope Lela was able to escape before this happened. If not, then my worst fears have come to pass. I was a coward. I should have stayed. I should have fought. But I'm nothing. I'm worthless. A pathetic waste of humanity. I don't deserve to exist. Everyone would be better off without me. Maybe if I hadn't been such a burden, my father wouldn't have turned out like he had. It's so fucking stupid. I tried to keep all my pieces together. Used the jacket as armor. He always wanted me to be strong, but I couldn't. I tried. I faked it. In the end I failed. In trying to be strong, I destroyed everything around me. Betrayed and hurt those who cared most. The Thompson's took a chance on me and I repaid them by punching Blake.

Blake. He was always there for me. And I was never there for him. Clarity. For the first time in probably forever, I can see all the mistakes I've made that put me where I am now. I don't have any options left.

Glass crunches under foot. I'm sure some of it has always been there, but it's hard to say for certain. What few family photos we had are smashed and torn. A tornado would have done less damage. Bending down I retrieve a picture. Somehow it survived, left as a reminder of what was lost. My father and I on a boat. His arm slung across my shoulders, the other holding a beer aloft in celebration of the fish I held up on a line. We're both smiling. Slightly sunburnt but happy nonetheless. I remember that day, but the feelings are lost now, buried under the detritus of my life. It was a good day, that much I know. It was a friend of my father's, former friend by now. He took us, a cooler of beer, sandwiches, and soda, all out on the lake and his beloved boat. The freedom of bobbing on the waves, our fishing lines dangling in the water. The air full of stories of those crazy life experiences created through the years. Each story tinged with regret covered by humor, an explosive laugh to fight against the failure of missed opportunities. As the day progressed, the stories became more outlandish. Fish bigger than a horse and sex in the backseats of cars. Their prowess exaggerated to godlike proportions. I didn't speak, just listened, a big grin on my face as our fishing lines lay slack in the water.

Tears trail down my cheeks to dampen the photo. We only caught one fish that day. My father sang my praises for that catch. Insisting his friend take a picture of us so that everyone would know I wasn't a complete failure. He forgot the moment days later, but the kernel of pride, of having caught my father's favor, stayed with me through a few beatings. But like everything else, it crumbled before his onslaught. I let the image fall, fluttering to rest among the destroyed remains of what once was before continuing my tour of regret.

Lela's phone peeks out from beneath an overturned chair. The chair has memories too, but like everything else, my father forgot them. It was his mother's. Once part of a set, it was the only one that had survived the years. The others broke under my father's rage or just from use. Now this one too is gone. Clearing the debris, I rescue the phone. The screen is cracked and dark. With a sinking feeling, I notice the small spot of dried blood marring the cover. Lela never escaped and I left her. Images of her body, lifeless and bloated from the elements, swim through my mind. I wonder if they'll ever find her. Will they find me? I hope they do find her somewhere. Her family, whomever they are, should know. Without thinking, I pocket the phone where it snuggles next to mine. Fitting that we will both die here. Will I suffer like she did?

Each step. Each stair, I draw closer to the end. I should write a note, but notes are for those who care and are left behind. I have none of these things. Blake. He'll never want to see me again. Brit too when she finds out what I've done. This knowledge hollows me out. Their hatred of me is easier to palate than their sorrow.

My room, once my sanctuary, lies in ruin. Every precious thing carefully demolished. Thought went into this destruction. This wasn't the blind rage of downstairs. This was the cold rage of calculated decisions. It was meant to hurt me. The duffel lies amid the wreckage. Its contents scattered across the room. My meager savings gone. Yet another thing my father stole from me. I should be angry at him, but even that is too much effort. I only have the strength for one final act.

I find a scrap of paper, a torn fragment of a book. Thankfully it's mostly blank. I waste time searching for a pen and find one jammed into the gap behind a desk drawer. Taking it with me, I stagger down the hall. Fear and anticipation bubble within me. I try to push it away, but even still, my hands shake when I start the tub filling. In a scattered scrawl, I write the only thing I can say now. I'm sorry. It has to be enough.

Tears again, hot against my skin. I can't stop crying, the world blurring into streaks of shades of black and white. The razor blade I hid years ago is still in its place behind the drain trap under the sink, a piece of duct tape encasing my freedom. I kept it there knowing that one day, I would use it and end my miserable existence. The case is small, but what it holds is so much more.

I carefully undress, folding each piece as if it were the most precious of cloth and not faded and worn. I'm stalling, but I can't force myself to move faster. I need to make things perfect. Resting my note on top of the careful stack, I turn towards the tub. My heart hammers in my chest. The case, holding its deadly cargo, trembles in my hand as I slide carefully into the hot water.

A small sigh escapes my lips as I slip into the near-scalding water. I didn't realize how tight my muscles are until they start to loosen. The small case lies on the edge of the tub. There, but not forgotten. I close my eyes and lean back, letting the hot water relax me. I have time, not to think, but to be. Exist only in the moment and not feel anything. No fear. No pain. No regrets.

When I'm finally relaxed, my hand finds the small case on edge of the tub. I push the small tab on the side, and it exposes its precious cargo. I open my eyes and, for the first time, look upon the end. Amazing that such a small thing could do so much. The blade is smaller than my thumb, its edge thin and sharp. I rescued the case from the school parking lot and hid it in the bathroom. At the time, I didn't think about it, but somewhere deep inside of me, I knew.

I turn the blade in my hands, the light from the bathroom window glimmering off its polished surface. The edge is keen and unblemished. I doubt it has ever been used. Fitting its first time will be to taste human flesh and blood.

My life is reflected in the metal as it turns in the dim light. All the pain. All the hurt. Soon to be cut from my body to mix with the water. My hand trembles as I lower the blade to my arm. I press the point so that it dimples the tender flesh of my wrist. Just a little more pressure and the skin will split. My hand freezes and refuses to move. Some buried sadistic part of me doesn't want me to end my worthless life.

"Fuck!" The word explodes out of me as I hurl the blade across the bathroom.

I bury my face in my hands and cry. I'm too much of a coward. Too fucking stupid to even die right. Eventually the tears stop, leaving me drained and tired. I slump back against the tub, my body slowly floating in the cooling water. It would be so easy to slip under the water and just stop. Let the water fill my lungs. But that too requires pain, a willingness to suffer. I'm tired of pain. My death shouldn't hurt. I've been beat up enough.

My phone rings from my pile of clothing on the toilet seat. I curse loudly as I emerge from the tub, water cascading down my body and onto the cheap bathmat. Dripping, I dig through my clothes. I manage to hit the talk button before it switches to voicemail.

"Hello," I croak into the receiver.

"Julius?" Brit's voice sounds worried. "Oh my god, are you ok?"

I clear my throat. "Yes…" with a sigh I slump onto the floor and lean against the cold porcelain tub. "No." I bury my face in my arm, forcing the tears back. My voice still shakes. "Everything sucks. I…I don't know what to do."

"Where are you?"

"I'm at home." I say quietly, tears are streaming down my face.

"It's ok, Julius." Brit says, her voice calm and sure. "I'll be right over. Just stay put. Ok?"

"Ok." I stammer. "But what if my dad comes shows up?"

Brit snorts. "Is he there now?"

"No."

"Then I doubt he'll be home anytime soon. If he shows up, we'll deal with him."

We. It's always just been me dealing with my father, never a we. It feels good to not be the only one this time because I doubt I could deal with him right now. Not like this. Not by myself. Lela tried to help but that just made things worse.

Brit hangs up after making me promise not to go anywhere. Like I have anywhere to go right now. I drag myself to my feet. I listen to the drain gurgle as I slowly get dressed. With trembling figures, I pluck the small blade from the floor and return it to its hiding place under the sink.

CHAPTER TWENTY-FIVE

Brit finds me sitting on the couch in the twilight of the living room. She doesn't say anything. I know what she sees, me, a pathetic excuse for a person surrounded by ruin. Despite the disgusting carpet, she kneels in front of me holding my cold and water wrinkled fingers in her warm soft hands. Eyes full of pity, she stares up at my tear stained face. I don't want pity. Don't deserve it. Pity is for people who are better than me. Who don't abandon the people they love. Guilt presses down on me. I should have stayed and protected Lela. I shouldn't have taken out my failures on my best friend. It's all my fault. Why can't she see that?

I try to pull away, but she holds on tighter. Her kindness burns my fingers where we touch. She doesn't ask me why I'm soaking wet or why I'm sitting in the dark. It's a good thing too because if she did ask, I'd tell her everything. The shame, the fear, the razor. If I say it, she'll know how horrible I really am. Maybe she'll leave. I don't want her to leave.

Brit releases my hands and wraps me in a hug. I shrink into the comfort of her arms. My tears soak the fabric of her coat. Eventually, I stop blubbering and take deep shaking breaths to calm myself.

"Let's get out of here," Brit says as she releases me and wipes a couple tears from my face.

I nod, not trusting my voice.

Brit bundles me up in her mom's car, a sensible four-door sedan. Normally, I'd say something obnoxious, but at the moment those kinds of things float through my head and disappear without going anywhere. The car starts moving and I huddle down further into my coat. I don't care where we go. The further away from my house the better. It holds too many memories and bad decisions. The memory of the cold, sharp, steel pressing against my skin makes my wrist itch. I was so close, yet I don't have the guts to go through with it. Not sure if I should be relieved or mad. Both feelings vie for attention, I just don't have the energy to feel.

The world blurs into multicolored streaks as tears once again fill my eyes. Brit rests her hand lightly on my arm. Her touch is both pain and comfort in the maelstrom of emotions scouring my soul. I take it all into me, letting it spread through my whole body, warming and freezing. I grab her hand, holding on like a lifeline. I'm scared I might break apart into tiny pieces and disappear.

Pulling off the road, Brit pulls onto a levee, rocks and snow crunching under the tires. The Wellsville reservoir is spread out below us, the water dark and muddy. We're on a ridge above it. If I jump, the current could pull me under never to be found again. The overlook is secluded and a favorite spot for couples looking for a little privacy. With the colder temperatures though, we're the only ones out here.

Brit looks at me for a moment before disentangling her hand from mine and climbing out of the car. I follow with a confused look on my face. Snow dusts my shoulders as she closes the distance between us.

Without another word, Brit takes my hand and leads me into the backseat. She pulls me tight against her and rests her cheek on my head. I feel small and safe. For the first time in forever, I don't feel like I'm about to fall apart. A shuddering sigh pulls from deep inside drawing all the pain and fear with it.

"What's going on?"

"I'm tired." I don't have the energy to say more. Besides, Brit doesn't need to know the gory details of my life. The mess I've made of everything. Lela.

She sighs. "You hit Blake." Her words slam into me like a freight train.

"I know." The tears threaten and I fight like hell to keep them back. I'm tired of being weak.

"I just wish you would talk to me. You ran off and then I don't hear from you until I get a call from Marcus saying you hit my brother."

Her pain presses against my walls. I want to talk to her, but I don't know what to say. Nothing in my head makes sense anymore. There are too many secrets piling up.

Pushing me away, she makes me look her in the eyes. "We've known each other a long time. Why can't you trust me? Why can't you trust Blake? Whatever is going on, you are not alone."

"Trust?" The word explodes from me as my numbness turns to rage. "Every time I trust someone, things go to hell and quick!"

My body shakes with unspent rage. Brit doesn't let go though. She sees through the wall of anger and it terrifies me. Part of me wants to hurt her just so she stops caring. I don't want her to see inside me. If she does, she'll see just how horrible I really am. I should run, but at the same time I want to kiss her. The revelation is shocking and before I can stop myself I quickly close the distance between us and smash my lips against hers. She pushes against me a moment before relaxing into the kiss. Her body softens against mine. Her breathing is quick and shallow and her heart pounds through the soft cotton of her shirt.

Brit's hands run up my chest and she grips my shoulders. Her lips harden against mine a split-second before she shoves me back against the door. My head cracks against the glass, dazing me for a moment.

"You bastard!" she says, her voice breathy. "You don't get to play that game with me." Her eyes are shiny with tears.

I blink, confused. The memory of the kiss still lingering on my lips.

"What?"

"You can't use me to feel better, dammit!"

My face hardens. That isn't why I kissed her. I run a shaking hand through my hair. Brit hugs herself, silent tears leaving tracks down her cheeks. She presses into the corner of the backseat putting as much distance as she can from me.

I breathe a shuddering sigh. "It's not like that."

It's my turn to look uncertain as she glares at me. My breath catches in my throat. I capture the image of her in my head, her eyes shining, her face vulnerable. I want to break the wall building between us, wrap my arms around her and hold tight. Protect her from the pain in the world and never let go. The strength of the emotion is staggering.

"I…"

"You hurt him," she interrupts, and the moment explodes and I crash down to reality.

My heart breaks, my brain whirling with guilt and shame. It's my turn to press into the corner of the seat. I can't look at her anymore. I turn my head, resting my cheek against the cold window.

"He hurt me too."

I taste the lie the words leave my mouth. He's always been there for me. Never questioning the random late phone calls begging for a place to crash. Buying my pitiful explanations for the bruises.

"No, he didn't! He loves you!" Her voice cuts through me, sharper than any knife.

"Really? Because when I needed him, he wasn't there." My rational brain is losing the battle and I don't have the strength to stop myself. Anger fuels me. Without it, I wouldn't be able to keep moving.

Brit's face turns to stone. "He's always been there." Here words are soft but each syllable is bitten off.

"Well, because of Marcus I had to call…" I slam my teeth shut before I mention Lela.

The silence hangs between us. Her face is expectant, waiting to hear the rest of the sentence. Bile fills my throat and I scramble out the door and into the thickening snow.

Warm, gentle hands pull my hair back from my face as I sob and retch into the dirt. I try to push the hands away, but I don't have the strength. My stomach heaves as I empty every emotion out of me. I don't deserve love, or kindness. I hurt my best friend and abandoned Lela. I'm not even man enough to help her.

I cough and dry heave, my stomach empty, my soul scoured. Brit helps me stand and I lean bonelessly against her. She bundles me into the back seat and slides in next to me.

Leaning against the window, I try to gather my jumbled thoughts while she fishes around inside her small purse. Her hair has come loose from its ponytail and hangs limply around her face, partially hiding the red blotches on her cheeks. Snow drifts lazily around us. I resist the urge the push the hair behind her ear. Her eyelashes flutter as she searches methodically. With a slight smile, she pulls out a small pack of tissues and some mint gum.

Quietly, she cleans my face as the snow swirls around the car. I don't move, scared to break the moment. There is a beauty in the quiet between us.

"Why?" I ask.

"Why what?"

"Why are you being nice to me?" I huddle in on myself. "I'm a monster." The last is quiet, small.

Brit leans away from me and cocks her head to the side. Her face a mixture of emotions.

"No, you're not a monster," she says and continues to wipe snot and tears off my face.

"I hurt my best friend." I say, a pit opening in my chest. A voice whispers in my head reminding me of my other failures.

Brit sighs and leans back. Her warm breath brushes against my face. Her eyebrows draw down in concentration.

"That doesn't make you a monster," Brit says, her voice even and measured. "No matter what you think, you are not a bad person."

I sigh and Brit wrinkles her nose, putting a hand in front of her face.

"Seriously. Here. Chew this," she says handing me the gum. "Your breath completely reeks of puke and I can't keep talking to you with that stench melting my eyeballs."

I can't help it, I laugh a horse croak before taking the gum and chewing it quickly. With a grimace, she pulls a bottle of mouthwash from her purse. Like seriously, where does it all go? Mint fills my mouth overwhelming the vomit taste that had been lingering in it. Brit sighs, a smile playing over lips, and leans back against the door.

"You're beautiful." I can't believe I just said that. My cheeks burn.

Brit looks away, her smile evaporating. Not the response I'm expecting.

"I'm sorry. I shouldn't have said that. Not after what happened. Just forget it. Ok?" God, I'm such an idiot. Stupid mouth saying stupid stuff.

Brit refuses to look at me and my heart sinks.

"Not that. I just want it to be a real thing."

She turns to me and her eyes are large and pleading. Hoping that what I feel is real and not some phantom, transient emotion. She's scared, not of me or the monster in my head, but of me not being honest. She wants me to want her because of who she is and not as someone to make me feel better. Because she doesn't need me to feel whole. It's a piece to a puzzle I never realized was missing until it was there.

It's humbling and scary, but for the first time in my life, I'm not going to hide. Without a word, I just pull her close. At first she resists, but I'm patient and gentle as I pull her into the circle of my arms. Folding her up on my lap, her head tucked under my chin it's my turn to comfort her. It's the most natural thing in the world. There is no fear like I have with Lela. No guilt. I don't want the moment to end, but I know we'll have to return to the real world eventually. But until then, nothing matters but the two of us. The outside world is dim and distant through the fogged-up windows. I tilt her head up and cover her trembling lips with mine. This. This moment is real.

CHAPTER TWENTY-SIX

"I'm sorry I wigged out," I say for the seventeenth time as we leave the overlook.

Brit smiles and brushes her hand against my cheek. "I'm not the person you should be apologizing to."

"I'm sorry." Number eighteen.

Brit's hands tighten on the steering wheel. "Please stop apologizing. That won't fix it."

"I know. I just don't know what else to do," I say helplessly.

"Have you considered seeing someone? You know, like a counselor?" Brit asks. "I care about you, but I can't fix what's hurting you."

I snort. "Yeah, right. Only losers and idiots go to shrinks." At least that's what my dad always said.

It's a good thing I wear my seatbelt because at the moment, Brit slams on the brake and glares at me.

"Oh? So which am I? An idiot or a loser?" Brit yells, tears streaming down her face. She grips the steering wheel so tight her knuckles crack.

"What the hell are you talking about?" I fire back.

"Therapy, you asshole!" Brit never swears, the fact she did makes me take notice.

"That's not what I meant," I say lamely.

"Oh yeah? So what did you mean?"

Brit's voice stabs into me like a knife while I sit there stupidly.

"I was in therapy," she continues.

"But why?" I ask, my voice finally working. "Your parents are like the best people ever?"

Brit takes my hands. "It wasn't them," she says, tears forming in her eyes. "It was me."

The last is said so quietly I almost can't hear her. I turn toward her and touch her cheek lightly with my fingertips.

"What do you mean?"

Brit sits silently as my thumb lightly strokes her cheek, her eyes closed. She takes a shuddering breath.

"Blake always did things so easily. He was always the perfect one. I couldn't live up to his perfection."

"But you are perfect," I say, my thumb still lightly stroking her cheek.

Brit snorts. "No. I'm not," she says, taking my hand in both of hers.

"You are to me."

"Stop," Brit says, giving my hand a squeeze.

She stares at our hands for a while. Her face briefly illuminated as a car speeds by us.

"You're not the only one with scars," she says, her hands trembling.

She raises her eyes to mine, daring me to judge her. I don't.

"My mom found me in the bathroom," Brit starts up again. "I had taken a steak knife from the kitchen." She pauses and takes a deep breath. "I was cutting myself because I hadn't gotten straight A's on my report card. Blake always got perfect grades. Normally, I hid it. Used a kit to clean everything but I think a part of me wanted her to know."

I look away at the mention of Blake's name, unsure of what I feel about him.

"Sounds pretty stupid, I know," Brit says, interrupting my thoughts and drawing my attention back to her.

I touch her cheek again, sadness welling inside. "No," I choke out. "Not stupid."

I know where that pain comes from. It breaks my heart that

Brit would feel that. "I don't ever want you to feel that pain again," I manage to get out passed the lump pressing into my throat.

Brit stares deep into my eyes. "Then, don't turn into someone who would hurt me like that."

It sounds so simple when she says it like that. If only it was. Just talking about my feelings won't make the Monster go away. He'll still haunt me.

"I have good days," she continues. "And some days where I just want to hide from the world. Bad days and I have to make sure I stay away from anything sharp."

Images of the razor blade as it pressed against my skin fills my mind. There was a moment of exhilaration. I was in control of everything if only for a moment. The thought chills me.

"Not having a certain someone in my life, helps too." Leaning forward she kisses me on the cheek. "Greg didn't start out bad, but slowly he broke me down until he was in control." She pauses and drops her gaze to our hands. "You standing up for me helped me realize what was going on."

"So, I guess that makes me a hero then?" The lightness in my tone hides the anger the mention of his name brings.

Brit laughs and it fills the car before giving me a simmering look. "I'm not big on heroes and their fancy white horses. I much prefer the brooding bad boy type." She winks and my heart stops.

I'm still collecting my thoughts when the engine revs as Brit pulls back on the road again.

All the lights are off by the time we pull into the driveway. Blake's car is noticeably absent from its customary parking spot.

"Where's Blake?" I ask.

It's a little late for him to be out. Usually when I'm there he's in bed at a reasonable ten thirty. I try not to think about where he might be.

"He sometimes stays with Marcus when he's upset," Brit says casually.

Pieces fit together and I realize what was in front of my face the entire time. "So. Um. Him…and Marcus?"

Brit flashes a crooked smile. "What? No, silly. We're all cousins." She rolls her eyes.

"Oh." The word draws out of me and now I'm really confused.

Touching my arm, Brit says, "Yeah…"

She pauses. I can tell she wants to tell me more, but siblings and secrets. I don't know. The situation is weird and I'm sure she can see it on my face. I'm clueless.

Brit cocks an eyebrow. "I'm sorry. He wanted to tell you himself."

"So he can tell you, but doesn't trust me?" It comes out a little hot and Brit crosses her arms.

"Listen," her tone softens. "He made me promise not to tell you. Trust has nothing to do with it. Your life is a mess and he didn't want to add to it."

I hate that she's right, but it's true. Trust is a rare commodity in my life. Everyone I trust has let me down in one way or another. Maybe I need to be less of a jerk and try to be the friend Blake deserves instead of the leech that I am. Nodding, I follow Brit out into the cold. Our steps are muffled by the snow, but the hardwood floors aren't so forgiving. Thankfully, the adult Thompson's sleep heavily. I'd rather Brit not get into trouble because of me.

At the bottom of the stairs, I pull Brit to me and kiss her. She comes willingly and melts into me. Our breath mingles as I pull her tighter. My body wants her to stay, but I know she can't. Not only would her parents kill me, but so would Blake.

And Lela.

Just thinking of her freezes my blood. Brit, sensing the change, pulls back with a sigh.

"You ok?" She whispers breathlessly.

My shoulders slump. "No. Just…" I stop and wave my hand around my head. One day I might be brave enough to tell her all the gory details, but not tonight. I don't have the strength and I don't want to test whatever we have going on yet.

Brit hugs me tightly. "Get some sleep. We can talk tomorrow if you want. Ok?"

"Yeah."

Kissing me on the cheek Brit disappears upstairs. I stand there for a moment staring wistfully at the point where I imagine Brit's bedroom is before heading down to where my futon is waiting. I pull out my phone and Lela's tumbles out of my pocket. I try to power it on but the battery is dead. The crack on the screen shouldn't make it unusable but I won't know until the morning. I set it next to my phone and plug it in. It won't help me find Lela, but like many things, I can't let go of my past.

If only I had a time machine. I could go back and undo everything. Undo me. Maybe a giant delete button and just erase myself from the cosmos. Then I remember my promise to Brit that I wouldn't hurt her. The lid slams shut on the thoughts in my head. No use wasting my time on them. Those pointless pieces of drivel that float in my skull.

It feels good to finally lie down. My body sinks into the foam mattress. Thoughts of Brit float pleasantly through my head before being shattered apart by the growing list of stuff I have to get done. The never-ending list of crap that won't get done unless I do it.

Just once, I wish someone else could take care of things for me. Let me sit back and enjoy having nothing to do. Unfortunately, unlike fairy tales, there are no true happy endings. Nothing ever works right and the list keeps growing.

Lela follows me into my nightmares.

CHAPTER TWENTY-SEVEN

I'm rescued from dreams of fear and pain by the shrill ring of my phone drilling into my skull. I groan and look over at the clock. 7 a.m. Who the hell is calling me? The only people who would call me live in this house. The number is unknown. Probably a wrong number. I mute the ringer and let voicemail answer.

I haven't seen Blake since I wigged out. I need to apologize to him. I was a jerk. I'll swing by the shop today. Maybe get some work done. Mrs. T also wants me to talk to someone about what happened. She says it's my punishment for getting in trouble at school. Can't argue with her, she used to be a nurse. She's seen it all.

And to add to it, I'll have to fire a call to Felicia. I float on the moment of kissing Brit and force my brain from reliving the bad parts of that night. Brit just wants to be with me. No agendas, nothing. Just me.

The phone yells at me again. Same number. Damn. Whoever it is, they're persistent.

I jab the talk button. "Hello?"

"Bout time you answered your phone," Blake grumbles.

"Sorry," I mumble, still groggy from sleep. "Didn't recognize the number."

"Oh. Right." There is an embarrassed pause before he continues. "Anyway, can we talk?"

The moment I've been dreading has arrived and I'm only partially conscious. "Yeah. Let me get some coffee in my face-hole."

Blake chuckles. "Ever the eloquent one. I'll be over in a few minutes."

"Sounds like a plan," I manage around the lump in my throat. With a groan, I crawl out of bed. After a quick shower, I toss on some clothes and bound upstairs.

"Julius! My goodness, you just about scared me to death!" Mrs. T exclaims. "You're in a hurry."

"Sorry," I say, embarrassed.

"You hungry? I could make you some eggs or something."

"That would be great," I say, my stomach gurgling.

I breathe a sigh of relief that there is coffee and gratefully pour myself a cup, breathing in the heady aroma. Mrs. T smiles at me as I lean against the counter. She's worried, I can tell. She's in full on mom mode. Giving me a quick hug, she sets to gathering supplies from the fridge.

"I know you won't tell me what's going on, but we're here for you."

I mumble a thank you and keep my eyes averted. Just looking at her will break me to pieces and I've just managed to keep everything together.

Adding some diced ham to her famous scrambled eggs, she continues. "Brit tried to get me to make you go see someone." She says it casually, but I've been around her enough to know that she'll push me if she has to. And having been on the receiving end of that many times, I know it's easier if I not fight against it. Brit and Blake are very stubborn, but Mrs. T is more so.

"After I get done talking with Blake, I'll call Felicia and see if she can get me set up with something." Not too excited about talking to someone, but Mrs. T will drag me to an appointment if she has to.

She slides the eggs onto a plate and finishes it off with a dollop of sour cream. Heaven. Taking it from her, I sit at the table just in time for the door to open and Blake's heavy tread echoes down the hall. I wonder if he's as nervous as I am? Mrs. T gives him a big hug and a cup of coffee before slipping out of the room. I don't even bother to comment. She sees all and knows all.

The bruise, though small, is a reminder of what I did. We both look at each other, uncertain. For the first time, I don't know what to say and it seems he doesn't either. Of course, he could be waiting for me to apologize.

"So..." I pause. "I kind of suck."

Blake looks at me, his eyes round with surprise before he starts laughing. I'm so shocked I can't help but join in with him.

Wiping tears from his eyes, he says, "Of all the things you could have said..." He pauses, shaking his head and chuckling.

"I am sorry. I...have a lot going on."

Major understatement, but he doesn't prod. Just waits patiently for me to talk despite having his own things to say.

Taking a deep breath, I decide on the truth. At least part of it. "I wasn't the only one at my dad's house that night."

His head snaps up. "What do you mean?"

I stall by refilling my coffee mug. "Her name is Lela. She's...a friend."

Blake raises an eyebrow but doesn't intercede. I can only imagine what he's thinking. Does he know about me and Brit?

"I crashed at her place and she drove me to my dad's so I could get a few things." I leave out that I was planning on disappearing with her, but he doesn't need to know that. "Anyway," I pause again as the memory of that night threatens to overwhelm me. Fighting back the terror, I continue. "He woke up and attacked us. Lela was downstairs. I couldn't get to her."

"That's when you jumped out the window?"

Nodding, I hide my guilt. "I haven't been able to contact her since then either."

Blake grips my arm. "And you were worried and instead of talking to your best friend, you tried to knock my block off?"

"Yeah. Pretty much. Your sister reminded me that was a shitty thing for me to do."

Smirking he steals some of my eggs. "That would be Brit for ya."

"Well, if your dad was chasing you, I'm sure your friend is ok."

"I don't know. I was at my house before Brit picked me up. I found her phone."

Whipping out his phone he starts dialing. "I need to tell Marcus."

"NO!" I grab his phone and close the app. "Not yet. For all we know, she dropped her phone."

"Still..." He reaches for his phone and I let him. "Ok. Do you need a ride to her place?"

And the truth comes out. "I don't know where she lives...we... didn't go to her place." Shame reddens my cheeks and I want to crawl inside a hole.

Blake stares, his look unreadable. It's worse than judgment. It doesn't take much to put the pieces together and realized that we more than likely slept together. My appetite disappears and I shove my food in his direction. My stomach can't handle Mrs. T's cooking right now. Blake's eyes light up and he starts wolfing down the food.

I let him finish before I ask the question on my mind.

"So Brit mentioned that you wanted to tell me something. I noticed you and your dad have been a little weird towards each other."

I may be self-absorbed, but I'm not blind. Now that I'm not running for my life and picking glass out of my face, I can focus on other things.

Sighing, Blake slumps back. "I was going to tell you."

It's my turn to comfort my friend. "You don't have to tell me. I mean, I know Marcus is involved. At first I thought you guys..."

Blake chuckles. "Yeah, that would make family gatherings really awkward." Scratching the back of his neck, he looks so much younger. I've always thought of him as this big brother, but he's only a couple years older. This is a new Blake. He's uncertain.

"I don't know how to say this," he starts, the words halting.

"Everyone always expected me to take over the shop when my dad retires in a couple years. Hell, up until a few months ago, I thought so too."

"But now?"

"Now…" He pauses again and looks away. "I'm going out of state. There's a police academy. Top notch."

The words hang between us. I don't know what to say. My stomach drops. Blake. A cop?

"I've always wanted to help people. Like really help people." His eyes swing back to me and I know I'm one of those people.

"You've been one of my best friends for longer than I can remember. You've always been there for me." My heart is breaking but I have to keep talking. "You need to stop saving me from my shit. You have more important things in your life." My body trembles as I fight everything to keep the tears at bay. Crying will make me weak and I can't do that. Not now. I have things I have to do and dragging him through it would be selfish.

Blake makes a move to stand, his face stricken, but I hold out my hand to stop him.

"Listen. You have a life. You should live it. Your job isn't to keep me in one piece."

"Julius—"

I laugh. "Blake. I can do this. My life might be a train wreck, but that doesn't mean I can't do this."

Looking down at his hands, he sits there a moment. "What are you going to do?"

Gathering my courage, as shaky as it is, I give him a confident smile. "I'm going to find Lela." I shrug. "After that, I don't know." Turning, I head back downstairs, the glimmer of an idea in my head. I hear the scrape of a chair followed by Blake's footsteps, but instead of heading towards the door, they follow me down. With an inward sigh, I check Lela's phone. My hands shake a little. If this works, I'll see her again. I don't know what I'll say or do when that happens. Life is more complicated than it was a couple days ago.

"What are you doing?" He asks, looking over my shoulder.

"This is her phone." The screen lights up and I let out a breath. "Most people don't disable location information. I'm hoping she didn't bother and I might be able to find out where she lives."

Scrolling through the apps, I find her map program. The urge to snoop into the rest of her life is overwhelming, but I'd rather not Blake see anything on there involving me. Not only would it start a series of uncomfortable questions, but this is her life. I won't talk about her to someone else without her knowledge. My hand trembles and I accidentally open her image folder. My blood freezes as the first image shows me sleeping in the hotel room, my naked chest partially exposed. My face is peaceful despite the bruises mottling my skin.

"The hell?" Blake exclaims, his breath puffing against my ear. Before I can react, he grabs the phone from my hand and starts scrolling. his eyes hard and his face a mask of fury and disgust.

"Please. Don't." The world blurs as tears fall from my face. "Blake. Stop!"

"Julius, what is going on?" Shock. Horror. Anger. All play across his face, punctuated by the light of the screen.

"It's not what you think," I sob.

He jabs the phone in my face. "How is this not what I think?" The image is slightly blurry from movement, but it's obviously me and Lela. There is no doubt as to what we might be doing. None.

Wrenching the phone away from him, I close the app with trembling fingers. Too ashamed to even answer him. I've never seen Blake this angry, but I deserve it.

"I need to call Marcus," he says, a wild look in his eye.

"No."

He stops and I stare him straight in the eye.

"No. I need to make sure she's ok first. No matter what has happened, I couldn't live with myself if my father has hurt her."

Taking a deep breathe, he nods. "Fine. But after that, I'm calling Marcus."

Without agreeing with him, I pull up the map and start tracing her life. For once, my luck seems to be holding out in this regard because she hasn't disabled her location settings. All roads lead to Rome, or in this case, a house out in the middle of nowhere.

CHAPTER TWENTY-EIGHT

A big green grain silo comes into view as we near where Lela's phone indicates she lives. We left pavement a while back and a plume of dust out flows out behind us like a tail. Rocks ping on the under carriage of the car as the tires slip and bounce over the dirt road. Blake hasn't said much the whole way over. All my attempts to engage him fail. Depression looms up at my failure. I wanted to be the hero, to make up for all my mistakes and now Blake knows. And when we find Lela, he's going to turn her in. Her life will be over and it'll be my fault.

I promised I wouldn't tell.

The house is two stories with an old style wrap-around porch. A worn picket fence surrounds the property separating it from rolling hills and cultivated fields. Like a lot of houses around here, it's seen better days, but with a little work, it could be a really nice place. Bigger than what I live in, that's for sure. If I had let Lela take me here that night, I wouldn't need to use her phone to find it. Blake would never have found out.

A small detached garage peeks out from behind. The door is closed and I think I spy the outline of a car, but the windows are too dirty for me to see. Hope fills me that she's home, alive and well, and just hiding out from my father. Not knowing what's going on because I have her phone.

We pull in the drive and Blake creeps up to the house. I try coming up with a plan, but everything I can think of sounds stupid. All I have is, go up to the door, knock, and see where it goes from there. If Lela is there, maybe I can convince Blake to leave her alone. There were times I said yes and others where I didn't say no even when I wanted to.

The house looks empty, but that doesn't mean someone isn't there. Parking the car, he lets out a slow breath.

"I'm sorry I wigged out," he says after a moment. "If I had known I could have done something."

Shaking my head, I grip his arm. "If I had been a better friend, I would have trusted you. But I didn't..." I stop at a loss for words. "I wish I could explain it, but I can't. What we had—"

"What you had wasn't a relationship," he interrupts. "What she did was wrong. Period."

Turning away, I wrap my arms around my stomach. I can't tell him that sometimes it didn't feel wrong. It felt amazing. I felt loved. Wanted. Needed. She never acted like they tell us about us in school. The first time it happened, I just wanted her to feel better. She was alone. Hurt. Afraid. The more it happened, the less weird it felt. Or maybe I just wanted it to be ok. Now, I don't know. The pictures haunt me. Based on Blake's reaction to them, they all included me in some form of undress. I knew about some of them. She asked. She told me it made her happy. The others, she didn't ask and never told me about. I don't have the courage to look at them all.

"I need some air," I croak out as I stumble from the car before resting against the door.

After a moment, Blake joins me and leans up next to me, our shoulders nearly touching. He doesn't say a word, just stares at the house and like me, processing the revelation of just how fucked up my life really is. Once again, he won't let me enter a lion's den alone. We might not be friends after this, but for the moment, he's there.

Bumping his shoulder, I steel myself as I lead us up the front steps. My heart hammers in my chest and my hands tremble as I reach for the door. I keep imagining me opening the door and catching a baseball bat in the face. It's doubtful my father's here.

For all I know he left town, but I can't top the gnawing worry that something bad is going to happen. As ridiculous as it sounds, I can't stop myself. I don't bother with the doorbell and try the nob. Surprisingly, it's unlocked. Easing the door open, we slip into the house. The front room is dim, and it takes my eyes a second to adjust. The walls are covered in old photos and Americana memorabilia. I'm no interior decorator, but even so the effect is jarring. The living room where I entered is a maze of furniture. Stacks of old books and magazines are scattered around making the spacious room feel cramped.

I turn and look at Blake. Of all the scenarios, I never expected Lela to live in a place like this. It's not that she was ever a clean freak, but it never occurred to me that she would horde things. Straining my ears, I don't hear anything beyond Blake's and my breathing. The house is quiet and empty.

Moving slowly through what I can only assume was once the family room, I leave Blake to stand bewildered in the middle of the room. Frankly, I'm surprised I'm as calm as I am.

"Are you sure this is the right place?" Blake's voice is loud in the hushed space causing me to jump. Stumbling, I bump into a stack of books which crashes to the floor.

With a silent curse, I check the phone again and confirm our location. "Yes," I say, my own voice muted.

Blake picks his way towards me. "Why are you whispering?" He asks, his tone matching mine.

"I don't know," I say a little louder. "It just feels weird and we don't know who is here."

"What aren't you telling me?" He searches my face.

"Nothing," I reply, meeting his gaze. "But they haven't found my father and there's no guarantee he isn't hiding somewhere. If he knew about this place, he might have come here."

Blake gives me a confused look. "Why would he know about this place? I thought she was your friend."

"And she was my father's girlfriend at one point."

The look he gives me can only be described as shocked. He doesn't say anything which is probably a good thing because I'd rather not have to be judged by him. Not right now. Right now, we need to find Lela. The longer we stay here, the more nervous I'm getting.

Entering the kitchen, we are greeted with more mess. Every flat surface is covered with stuff. So much so, it's overwhelming. The room reeks of garbage and rotting food from the pile of unwashed dishes and overflowing trash can. My stomach threatens to empty itself but I manage to keep everything down. It takes years to accumulate this much crap.

An aluminum can crunches underfoot, squirting a small amount of beer to mix with whatever else is coating the linoleum. I cast a disgusted glance down and freeze. Horror fills me.

"What's wrong?"

I look up. "Lou's Beer."

"What?"

"Lou's Beer. It's my dad's favorite."

Blake makes a disgusted face. "That stuff tastes like ass."

"I know and Lela hated the stuff. She would never have it..."

"Unless your father was here," Blake finishes. "Ok." He looks around. "Chances are he isn't here. We didn't see his car out front. Right?"

I nod, fighting the welling panic. "There was something in the garage, but I couldn't tell what it was. I don't think it was his. Shape was wrong."

"Right." He glances over. "I'm guessing that leads to the cellar." I see the door he's pointing at and based on its location it's either a cellar or a pantry as the stairs to the upper floor travel just above it.

"Doubt she's down there. Let's check upstairs and then get out of here quick."

"I'm texting Marcus." It's not a question and I don't stop him. If my father is here, having backup, especially police related, is probably a good thing.

"What should we do?" I'm scared—terrified really—and for the first time today, I don't know what to do. My father's been here and there's a good chance Lela is too. Why she hasn't tried to escape is beyond me, but knowing my father, he would find a way to keep her here and away from me. There is a good chance he knows about Lela and me. Better than a good chance. Deep down, I'm certain. Knowing him, he's kept her here. I just hope we're not too late. When he flies into a rage, he doesn't stop. He's choked me into unconsciousness before and I'm his son.

Blake grips my arm, anchoring me. "We search the house. We find Lela. We get the hell out of here."

"But what if he's here?"

"Then we fight."

I blink at him. Blake? Fight? He's never lifted a finger to anyone. Yeah, he played football and was damn good at it, but he was always a good sport. He'd knock someone down, then he'd help them stand. He was competitive, but never aggressively so.

His cheeks color. "When you called the other night, I was at the gym taking a kick-boxing class."

"Aerobics might get you in shape, but they aren't self-defense courses."

Chuckling, Blake gives me a sly grin. "Don't tell my dad, but Marcus introduced me to this guy who fights MMA. He's been teaching me a few things."

My eyes bulge, making him smirk. Definitely not someone to get on the wrong side of.

He pats me on the shoulder. "When this is over, I'll introduce you. Maybe get you in a few classes."

"I'm not sure that would be the best idea," I say as I navigate through the maze of stuff to the stairs leading up. "I'd rather not learn how to hurt someone."

"It's more than fighting, it's learning how to control your body. It's about balance and clearing your mind."

In another time and place, I'd make a crack about him being a dumb jock. Now, I'm too jittery and if I start laughing, I might not stop. Creaks and groans echo through the silent house with each step. Reminding me of the night Lela and I tried to sneak into my dad's house. I try walking as close to the wall as possible, but the stairs are just too old. If anybody is home, they've either heard us or they're dead.

The upstairs is just as messy. There are several doors leading off a single hallway that runs the length of the house. One door in particular catches my attention. Unlike the others, this one has a chair propped under the handle keeping it shut. Blake and I share a look. His eyes are wide. His face pale. There can be only one person that could be behind that door. My heart soars with relief and I hear muffled noises come from the other side. Lela is alive. But if she is in that room, where's my father?

I lightly tap on the door. "Lela? Is that you?"

The faint noises behind the door cease.

I tap again. "Lela? It's me, Julius."

Muffled sobs come through the door and I wrench the chair out of the way. Immediately the door flies open and Lela tumbles into my arms. Bruises decorate her skin. Her clothes are torn and dirty and with a start I realize they are the same ones she was wearing that night. Blood has soaked into her clothes from the various cuts and scratches. I don't even want to know the horror she has experienced.

"Oh baby," she cries. "You found me." She clutches at me like I'm the only thing keeping her alive.

"I'm so sorry," I say as hot tears scour my face. "I should have stayed but I was a coward."

Burying her face into my chest, she wraps her arms around me. "No. I would never have forgiven myself if he hurt you because of me."

I tilt her head up and swallow bile at the sight. One eye is swollen shut, a gash on her cheek is red and crusted with dried blood. Brushing a tear from her face, I fight the urge to kiss her. It's a trained response. This is not the first time I've seen her like this. She would tell me that being with me took all the hurt away. Two years later, I still want to.

"Marcus," Blake says into his phone, startling both of us. "We need an ambulance." Blake nods and hangs up. "He's on his way." Looking down at us, his anger softens. "Is Frank here?"

Lela shakes her head. "No. He left earlier, but I don't know where he went or when he'll be back."

"Ok. Can you walk?" I ask.

"I don't know."

Without a word, Blake reaches down and picks her up, cradling her gently in his arms. Tires crunch on gravel and we all freeze. When a car door slams, Lela starts to panic. Blake tries to sooth her, but I heard the sound the door made. It wasn't the smooth thump of a newer car, but rather the metal on rust scream that my dad's car makes. With a worried look over Lela's head, I make a shushing gesture as I lead us to the stairs. I'm dead certain it's my father. He knows someone is here and we'll have to fight through him if we want to get Lela to safety.

CHAPTER TWENTY-NINE

A thump followed by the sound of crackling safety glass stops us in our tracks. It happens again and is shortly followed by the sound of crunching metal. Blake's car. My father must recognize it and what it means. It's the only explanation at this point. After what seems like an eternity, it stops. Blake glances over at me, his eyes wide. I imagine he sees the same look in mine.

I peak down the stairs and don't see anything but the door, wide open the way we left it. Sunlight dapples the floor, illuminating the dust motes in the air. Motioning him forward, we creep downstairs. The house is quiet and I keep glancing around to make sure he's not sneaking up on us. Blake sets Lela on her feet and she immediately stumbles as her legs buckle. Catching her, I hold her close, taking her weight. Together, we shuffle behind Blake, his body like a shield.

We catch a view of his car through the open door. Most of the windows have been broken and several large dents pepper its once pristine exterior. It breaks my heart, but it's all we have. There is no sign of my father and Blake lets out a relieved sigh before glancing back at us.

A shadow blocks out the sun. Seeing the fear dawning on my face Blake turns. The world slows to crawl and I can only stand and watch, my body frozen, as my father's old baseball crashes into Blake's forehead with a sickening crunch. The half rotten wood splinters sending a piece flying off to the side. Blake's body vibrates with the force of the hit before crashing to the floor, his limbs twitching. Lela screams and pulls away from me before her weakened legs collapse. Throwing away the now useless bat, my father glares at us. With a cruel twist of his lips, he kicks Blake's ribs. The sound is dull, hollow and Blake doesn't make a move.

"This is what you get for taking Missy away from me!" He roars before his eyes travel back to me where I'm helping Lela stand again.

Missy. Missy was my mom. Blake helped her leave? No. He would have been too young. But his parents weren't. I barely register the betrayal as I desperately try to reconcile that my best friend might be dead and my father doesn't want to stop with him.

Clenching his fists, my father steps over Blake's still form and advances on us. Each step slow and deliberate. Hindered as I am with helping Lela, his steady progress brings him closer and closer. At this rate, he'll get us before we reach the stairs and he knows it. He knows I won't leave her again.

"Leave me," Lela whispers.

"No." Tears fill my vision and my father grins at my weakness.

"Run!" Lela yells before pushing away from me and crashing into my father in a tangle of limbs.

Once again, I run while she's left behind. Lela cries out with the sound of my father's fist hitting flesh. Putting my guilt into a tiny box, I duck into the room where we found Lela. Thankfully, the door is open, but I know it won't save me for long. Lela cries out a couple more times before I slam the door shut. All the furniture is heavy oak. If I can slide a piece in front of the door, I might be able to survive.

Spying an old vanity, I plant my shoulder on the side and give it a shove. It moves an inch before catching on a rug. Cursing, I shove it again. It slides another inch, the rug bunching up more. The floor shakes as my father stomps up the stairs. I give it another desperate shove and it tilts on the rug before crashing over in front of the door. The mirror explodes, sending glass fragments flying across the room. I stand there panting, my muscles trembling from exhaustion and fear. It won't slow him down much, but maybe enough.

The wall shudders as my father's body slams into the door. The downed vanity shifts and my dad smashes into the door again. Adding my weight, I struggle to keep it from moving any more. The violence of his assault on the door continues and each blow rattles my teeth and pushes me closer to the bed. The window beckons. I've done it before, but this is higher. I might survive, but I won't be able to walk away. The only hope I have is that a miracle happens, or he runs out of steam. With a roar he hits the door like a battering ram sending me flying into the bed.

"You won't take her away from me!" my father, the Monster, screams from the door.

My own anger swells within me. "I had nothing to do with this!" I shout back.

He stands in all his raging glory, his face and clothes splattered with the blood of his victims, eyes red and wild. The smell of stale sweat and alcohol washes over me. I know in that instant he could kill me and not even blink. With cold certainty, I realize this was my fate the moment I didn't leave with Lela.

Forcing myself to calm my frantic heartbeat, I try the logic approach. I can't fight him. He's too strong, too crazy. But maybe I can buy some more time.

"Dad." I say, hoping he isn't beyond reason. "Please. Let's talk about this." I move slowly to my feet and quickly scan for a weapon.

"No!" My father roars smashing the fist into the door, splintering the doorjam with a loud crack. I can't imagine the damage it's doing to his hands.

"Please! It doesn't have to be this way!"

"Shut up," My father screams. "This is all your fucking fault!"

I slowly back out of reach. "Dad. Please." I beg.

His gaze swivels to me. "You! I did this all for you! You ungrateful little shit!"

"Dad." I'm hoping if I remind him that he's my father, I won't die. "Listen, I'm sorry. Just calm down so we can talk. Ok?"

My father rushes me and slams me up against the wall, knocking a picture to the guard, the glass front shattering. I manage to get my hands up in time to keep the him from crushing my neck as he pushes his forearm under my chin.

"I did it for you!" He screams, his fetid breath washing over me, his spittle splattering on my face.

I try and talk but his arm is pressing against my throat cutting off my air. It's all I can do to keep it from pressing harder. My arms shake with the effort. I've never tested my strength against my father. It isn't enough. I'm going to die.

"Everything I did was for you and what happens? My own son bangs my girlfriend!"

Tears are streaming down my face. I try to speak, but I can only gasp for air as my vision starts to darken at the edges as the room wavers.

"Don't fucking lie to me! I know you did it! You and the goddamn Thompsons trying to screw me over and take what's mine. Just like your mother."

If I don't do something soon, it will all be over. I ram my knee as hard as I can between his legs. He roars and stumbles back, grabbing his crotch. My rage explodes in my head and I attack. My fist connects with the side of his head and pain explodes up my arm. Despite its ultimate futility, I continue my desperate assault. Maybe I'll get lucky and hit just the right spot to take him out but I know that won't happen.

With an insane cry, my father crashes into my side carrying us both into the hallway. My head smacks into the wall dazing me. My father's fist smashes into the side of my face making the stars dance before my eyes.

He screams incoherently as his fists pummel me. Curling into a ball I cover my head from his savage attack. He takes advantage of the opening to my stomach and drives his booted foot into my ribs driving the air from my lungs. Bones crack under the force. My vision blackens as pain knifes through my chest. Everything goes numb, my body beyond pain. Even if I wanted to, I wouldn't be able stop him. My heart breaks. He truly is lost to me, his mind consumed by rage. I'm not his son anymore. Maybe I never was.

I hear a muffled shout, and my father's assault pauses for a moment. Lela claws at his face and arms. He swats her with his arm like a fly and, weakened as she is, she crumples. He stands over her, his hands raw and bloody. His chest heaves from exertion and anger. I try to stand, but my body doesn't respond. Each breath scrapes my lungs and my ribs shift in a way that they shouldn't. My head throbs with each beat of my heart. The world wavers.

"You whore!" He yells grabbing Lela by the neck and slamming her against the wall. "You think you can take me?" He spits into her face. His voice, strangely muffled.

I'm dying. I know it. My heart aches for the pain I know Brit will feel. Tears course down my ravaged face. I'll never be able to tell her how she makes me feel. How important she is or that her brother tried to save me.

My father drops Lela and she falls bonelessly to the floor. Her legs giving little twitches. I hope she's still alive. She doesn't deserve to die, nor does she deserve the pain inflicted on her. She's made her own mistakes, but she only wanted to be loved. I won't hate her for that. My father though. None of us knew what he was capable of. Or maybe I did and just didn't want to see it. In my effort to survive day to day, I closed my eyes to the monster in front of me. So many regrets but it doesn't matter anymore. My father turns his angry gaze back on me. Reaching down, he lifts me up by the neck. It's my turn to have the very breath squeezed out of my lungs. Anger wells up, giving me a spark of energy. I desperately try to loosen at his fingers. Only one arm manages to weakly pull at his thick, calloused fingers. The other just hangs there unmoving. He's yelling at me, but I can't hear him from the roaring in my ears.

My body starts twitching as my brain misfires from the lack of oxygen. The world narrows down into a bright point. This is the end. I just wish I could have said goodbye to Brit and Blake. They've always been there for me, never asking for anything in return. I whisper a silent apology to both of them and give in to the encroaching darkness.

The pressure on my neck disappears and I'm falling. It isn't until I hit the ground and pain arcs through my chest that I realize I'm not dead. Light and sound crash back into the world and I take a gulping breath. A writhing mass of shadows ricochets down the hall. Several voices are all shouting and cursing.

I hear the sound of crackling electricity followed by silence. Heavy breathing and muttered curses fill the void. A face slides into view, concern etched on its features. I see a flash of silver on a blue shirt. I breathe a shuddering sigh of relief as the police officer calls over their shoulder to get the paramedics.

I slide into oblivion. I'm alive. I'm alive. I'm alive.

CHAPTER THIRTY

Consciousness comes slowly but Brit's there when I wake up. The sterile walls of a hospital room greet me. My body throbs with pain but it lacks the intensity I would expect. Everything is floaty and hazy, but that's ok. I'm alive. A tight band encircles my chest and my breath comes short and painful. The heart monitor beeps steadily. I smile at Brit, or at least attempt to. The bandages covering my head and the meds coursing through my system make moving awkward.

She smiles back to me, tears forming at the corners of her eyes. Through force of will, I manage to get my arm moving. I try to wipe the tears away, but only succeed in bumping weakly into her face. Grabbing my hands in both of hers, she kisses my knuckles as more tears fall. She looks worn and tired, her hair in disarray, but she's more beautiful than anything.

"Hey," I croak.

Brit rests her check against my hand. "Hey."

"If you get snot on my hand, you're gonna have to clean it up."

Brit snorts in quiet laughter and kisses my knuckles again.

"How bad is it?"

Brit rubs her cheek softly against my hand. "The doctors say you should be able to get out in a few days," she says. "They want to make sure you're…" Her face is drawn, her eyes clouded with grief. Scenes from the attack rush forward and I ask the question I'm scared to know the answer to.

185

"Blake?" A part of me wants to ask about Lela, but I don't know how to form those words.

She shakes her head, her face twisted in grief. My stomach falls and I try to twine my fingers with her, but my fine motor control is shot. She gets the idea and helps.

After a moment, she speaks. "They don't know. He's stable, but he was hit really hard. If he wakes up...." Her voice breaks. "If he wakes up, he may never be the same."

"I'm sorry. My fault."

Laying her head on my shoulder, she wraps her arms around me. "Not your fault, you big dummy. I know Blake would have gone whether you asked him or not."

Nodding, I don't tell her the real reason he went. That he insisted because he didn't trust me not to disappear with Lela. Anger flairs up in me and the heart monitor beeps in sympathy. He didn't trust me. But as quick as it hits, the reality crashes back in. If he hadn't come with me, then I would have been alone not only with Lela, but my father. He would have hit me instead of Blake. My best friend saved me and bought enough time for the police to arrive.

"Where Marcus?" I hate that I can't make complete sentences, but a swollen face and heavy sedation will do that. I'm surprised I'm not seeing pink elephants float across the ceiling.

"With Blake. He hasn't left his side since the paramedics wheeled him in."

"He probably hates me." The longer I'm awake, the easier talking is getting. Still feels like wads of gum are glommed to my cheeks.

She squeezes me tighter. "Nobody hates you, Julius." Pulling back, she brings out the full force of her gaze. "I love you. Yes, you. Now stop putting yourself down." She leans over and kisses my lips lightly. The salt from her tears mixes with her chapstick in my mouth, a faint hint of strawberry. The heart monitor beeps faster as her kiss deepens. We're interrupted by polite cough and Brit jumps back.

"I see our patient is finally awake!" The nurse says brightly as she walks over to check on me. "How are we feeling today, Mr. Monroe?"

"Just Julius, please," I say quietly. "Mr. Monroe is my father."

A shadow crosses her face for moment before she smiles again. "Of course, Julius. I'll make a note in your chart."

"Thank you. If you have the number for the bus that ran over me, I'd appreciate it."

The nurse smiles at me. "Feeling better I take it."

Her gaze flits over toward Brit, who dips her head. The nurse, whose nametag reads Alice, sticks a thermometer under my tongue. It beeps and she pulls it out before writing the number down. She moves efficiently around the room chatting idly with me while she records my vitals and makes notes on my chart.

"Now Miss? I'm going to need you to leave. There are a couple gentlemen that want to talk to Julius and then the doctor wants to check up on him."

Brit's looks agast, but her eyes are smiling. She gives my hand a squeeze. "Don't go anywhere, Tiger." She gives me a wink as she walks out of the room. My eyes follow the sway of her hips, memorizing the shape of her.

"She's quite the looker," the nurse admits making me blush. "You're a lucky boy. She's been here since they wheeled you in. We tried to shoo her off, but she's a stubborn kid."

I smile at Alice. "That she is." The truth of that statement encompasses more than I could ever say.

Alice puts her hands on her hips and tilts her head to the side. Her slightly graying brown hair is pulled up and away from her face. "I've met her father" she says a smile cracking her olive skin. "You best be good to her or you might end up in my care again."

I try to laugh and it comes out as a wheeze that devolves into a painful cough. "Ow." I whisper as knives jab my ribs.

Alice's smile wavers a little and the lines at the corners of her eyes deepens. She pats my hand. "You try not to laugh too much, you have a couple broken ribs."

"That would explain why it feels like someone's stabbing a hot poker through my chest." It's an easy banter that helps take my mind off of everything, if only for a moment.

Alice smiles knowingly. "Are you up to visitors?"

I swallow and nod. Pressing a button on the bed remote, she raises me up into a sitting position. She adjusts the pillow and rolls a tray in front of me. On it is a small plastic pitcher with a cup of ice water on it.

"If you're hungry, I can get you a snack. Dinner will be ready in a couple hours. Ok?"

I manage to lift the cup to mouth and take a sip of water through the straw. "Thanks. That would be great."

"Alright. If you need anything, just press the call button next to you and someone will be here to help you."

"Thank you, Alice."

Alice smiles warmly. "Sure thing, hon. I'll be back in a bit with something to eat."

Alice leaves the room and a moment later a police officer and a detective enter, with a start I recognize Officer Romero. The sudden movement sends pain lacing through the warm blanket of the drugs

"Good afternoon, Mr. Monroe," she says. "I'd like to introduce Detective Jones."

Jones is a tall man with a smattering of gray in his close cropped, brown hair. Fine wrinkles crease his light skin. His eyes are a piercing blue that seem to follow even the slightest mistake. He wears a dark suit that makes him even more imposing. Instead of shaking my hand, which is half-encased in a cast, he nods his head.

"If you are up to it, we'd like to talk to you about what happened." His voice is soft, but holds a detached coolness that sends my nerves jangling.

Nodding, I take a sip of ice water, relishing in the cold as it soothes my throat. I'm sure it's just tap water, but at the moment, it is the best thing I've ever drank.

Jones starts by asking me a series of standard questions. What happened. Why was I there. Why we didn't call the police immediately. I do my best to answer. He asks about my father's relationship with Lela. Satisfied, he flips his notebook closed.

"Now do you have any questions?" He asks.

Do I ever. "Is Lela ok?"

"Ms. Menjaro is recovering," Jones responds.

"She was very lucky that you and your friend where there," Romero interjects.

Detective Jones frowns slightly, but doesn't correct her.

I don't ask about my father. I know they were able to arrest him. If he were dead, they would say something. I wish he was, but I know that isn't the solution. He's a monster, but I don't have to stoop to his level no matter how bad I want to smash his face with a brick for what he's done. Jones leaves Romero behind. She looks at me with a mixture of sadness and regret.

"I promised to keep you safe. I didn't live up to my side of the bargain."

I give an approximation of a comforting smile. "My father has a tendency to screw up people's plans."

She lets out a short laugh. "Well, we have him now and he's not getting out anytime soon." Her face turns serious. "I wish you had mentioned his girlfriend. But I understand. You were scared."

By the time they leave, I'm exhausted and empty. My father almost killed Blake. He'll be in jail for the rest of his life. Brit wanders back in and holds my hand as I tell her what the police said. Lela didn't deserve what happened to her. It tears my heart into pieces that she suffered so much. Brit gently wipes the tears from my face and carefully crawls up onto the bed with me and rests her head on my shoulder. It's a tight fit and the weight of her against my ribs is painful, but her comfort helps.

I must have dozed off like that because the next thing I realize Alice has returned with a plate of food and is staring at Brit with a slightly disapproving look. Brit gets off the bed, a guilty look on her face. My ribs ache, but it's nice having Brit there. I manage, with Brit's help, to eat the hospital food. Being down sucks, but at the same time, it's nice to be taken care of. Just wish the food tasted better.

Brit's parents show up and my heart clutches in my chest. Instead of anger for getting Blake hurt, Mrs. T brings me a bouquet of flowers that fill the room with their perfume. I'm floating in and out consciousness, by the time they finally decide leave. Brit wants to stay, but after a stern glare from her mother, relents.

"I'll be back tomorrow," Brit promises.

"After school," Mrs. T says pointedly, and Brit rolls her eyes.

"Fine! After school." She sounds upset, but she gives me a wink before kissing me firmly on the lips. "Bye, Tiger," she says a little breathlessly. I blush.

They dim the lights and I float off into drug induced nightmares full of rage and fear. But no matter what I try, I can't wake up. Eventually, those too fade and darkness consumes my mind.

"Hey, baby," Lela whispers into my ear, jolting me awake.

The heart monitor registers the spike before settling down to a slightly elevated rate. At first, I think it's a dream, but Lela looks almost as bad as I feel. Her voice is raspy and a plastic collar circles her neck.

"Hey," I finally manage. "I'm glad you're ok. When you fell…." I can't even finish the sentence. I don't tell her that a part of me hoped she was gone. Guilt washes over me at the thought. I don't want her to be gone, but her being around makes things way more complicated. I hate myself. She doesn't deserve that from me. Especially not after what she went through at my father's hands.

Reaching for my hand, she pauses, and when I don't flinch, takes my hand in hers. "It's ok, Jules." Her eyes well up and I want to hold her and make it all better, but I can't. Sensing this, she shakes her head and wipes her eyes clear. We were always in tune it seemed.

"What's wrong?" I ask. She's been through so much. We've been through hell together and I don't want her to be sad anymore. "My father can't hurt us anymore."

Lela lets out a choked sob and tears spatter on my hand. Her grip tightens painfully, but I don't move. Sometimes when she's really upset, she hurts so much. I don't want to cry, but I can't help it. I don't care if I look weak right now.

Noticing my tears, she touches my cheek. "Don't cry, baby. It's not your fault. It's mine. I…" She stops and takes a shuddering breath. "I have to go." The last is barely a whisper.

The words tear at me in ways that my father's fists couldn't. My soul and heart is shattered. I don't move. I can't speak. If I open my mouth, I'm scared of what I'll say. There is a part of me that doesn't want her to go and an equally forceful part that does. Ultimately, I know, deep down, she can't stay. If my father goes to trial, what secrets will he force out of us.

"Listen," she says, a slight tremor to her voice. "I do love you, but I know now I'm not good for you. What I have done is so wrong." She pauses again and I give her hand a squeeze.

"But…"

She silences me with a shake of her head. "Don't try and convince me. I had time to think while your father had me." Her voice gains strength as she continues. "I hurt you. Used you. And don't try to argue because I can see the fear in your eyes every time I look at you."

It breaks my heart, but she's right. I always thought I hid it well enough, but she knows me better than I ever knew.

"Where are you going?"

She boops my nose with her finger. "That's a secret. I can't have a certain brave young man chasing after me."

I shake my head. "I'm not brave. I'm weak."

Her eyes grow hard. "That's bullshit."

My eyes go wide, and my mouth hangs open.

"You are the bravest and strongest person I know. Your dad just convinced you that what you were thinking and feeling was wrong. It isn't."

Pulling her hand to my mouth I kiss it. "I'm not strong enough to keep you from leaving."

Leaning down, she brushes her lips against mine. "Baby, deep

191

down you know I can't stay. You have a life to live. One that doesn't include a horrible person like me. You deserve happy."

"I'll miss you."

She gives me a sad smile. "Don't come looking for me, Julius Monroe. And don't bother looking for me at the old house. It wasn't mine anyway. Just some place I was staying." Disentangling herself, she drifts over to the door. With a final look, she disappears.

CHAPTER THIRTY-ONE

After who knows how long, they finally let me get out of bed and move around. Apparently, I have metal pins in my right arm now to keep things together. Good thing too because I was getting restless and cranky. Muscles scream in protest, but I manage to support my own weight. Barely. Using the IV as a support and Alice as my guardian, I shuffle down the hall to Blake's room. ICU is on another floor and I wince as each jolt of the elevator, no matter how minor, sends a wave a pain through my ribs.

"Too bad the surgeon couldn't have removed the cracked ribs while he was fiddling around inside."

Alice laughs. "Unfortunately, they're kind of important."

"Yeah, well they suck right now," I say as the elevator comes to rest at Blake's floor.

"I'd think the arm would be in more pain."

I let out a wheeze, it's the closest thing I can get to a laugh that doesn't hurt. "Considering the metal in it now, I'm expecting to be able to lift cars when I get out of here."

That elicits another laugh from Alice and I decide that I like her. I always expect nurses to be cranky old ladies, but not her. No matter what, she's always smiling. It makes me a little jealous that she can be so light despite everything she must see.

She checks in with the nurse on station before leading me around to a room around the corner. Everywhere I look, I see people struggling to stay alive. The nurses here are more about efficiency than bed-side manner. They have to be, but it tears at me to know that Blake is in such a cold place. When we get to his room, Marcus is there. Tubes and wires connect to various machines to monitor Blake and keep him alive. He looks so small, his skin pale. A large, padded bandage encircles his head. Everything is hushed.

Marcus doesn't even register my presence, so intent on my friend to see the rest of the world. That too, breaks my heart. My father did more than steal my best friend. He also took my best friend away from his family. I don't have words to comfort him, so I sit in a chair opposite and take Blake's free hand. Alice backs out of the room before sliding the door partially shut.

"He always wanted to be a hero," Marcus finally says, his eyes still tracing every line of Blake's face. "He always suspected what your father did to you. It's why he wanted to be a cop."

His voice isn't accusing, but I feel the weight of it. I caused this. I could have found another way. Could have left with Lela. Escaped to another town. It would have been hell, but Blake would be awake and happy, teasing his little sister and being with the ones he loved.

"At first, I didn't like it. Hated it even." Now he looks at me and I'm hit full on with the depth of his feelings. "But then I met you." He lets out a wry chuckle. "You were a real ass that night, but I could see what Blake saw. The fear. But like Blake, I couldn't do anything without proof and you were so good at hiding it."

The weight of it all crushes down on me. "I'm so sorry," I manage to get out through the lump in my throat. "I never meant for any of this to happen, but I guess that doesn't mean much."

"Don't ever say that, Julius." His eyes bore through me. "Blake made the choice to be your friend. He made the choice to go with you." He pauses again and turns his eyes back to Blake. "Hell, I could take some of the blame myself. I hung up on you. I could tell you were freaked, but Blake needed to get his frustrations out. He and his dad had been fighting about him not taking over the shop. Don't get me wrong, his dad loved him, but he still struggled with Blake's choice."

"So you gave him the chance to be free of everything," I say, Deep down, I understand and a part of me is mad at him, but the rest gets it.

"Yeah. He was falling apart. He cared so much for other people. For you especially. I didn't get it. I thought you were just using him. So I encouraged him to leave."

Regret is a terrible thing. It's a weight that crushes you.

Tears spring in my eyes. "He was always a hero." The was fills the room. His choice to help me probably cost him everything.

"Man," Marcus says with a shake of his head. "He was pissed when he saw he missed your call. For a moment, I thought he might knock me into next week."

"Then he calmed down and felt bad about being mad. Right?"

The room fills with light as Marcus throws back his head and laughs. "That's about how it works."

Standing up, I let my friend go. "When he wakes up, I hope you're there."

Marcus looks at me serious. "What about you?"

"Me?" I ask as I hobble to the door. "I'll be around, but he needs his family more."

Nodding, Marcus turns back his vigil. I try to ignore the tears streaming down his face as he buries his head against Blake's chest. One day, Blake will wake up but I won't be the anchor that holds him back. It's time for me to stand on my own feet. Fight my own battles.

Marcus voice stops me at the door. "He always thought of you as family."

The air leaves my lungs and it's all I can do to make it out of the room before sobbing. I've always wanted to be a part of his family. In a way, I always was and I never realized. And now, Blake is fighting for his life because of me.

My father's house doesn't feel like my home anymore. Before I left the hospital, Felicia told me that I could pick up any of my things that I wanted. When the Thompson's picked me up and we all headed over. True to her word, Felicia and Alice meet us there. What I have isn't much. Most of my stuff went out of the window or got destroyed by my father's rage. Still, I need help and after a few directions, Mr. And Mrs. T round up what they can gather in my old room while Felicia and I wait downstairs. Alice assures me that she's just there as a witness to sign off that I got everything. The rest will stay with my father to do who knows what with. If he ever gets out of jail.

While no one is looking, I slip into the upstairs bathroom and retrieve the blade from under the sink. I'm not sure why, but it's still a part of me. When I come back down, I notice Felicia standing at the bottom of the stairs looking at the few photos from the broken pile of the floor. Most of the frames are the kind of crap you can buy at Wal-Mart. The stuff that looks fancy, but is just cardboard, glue, and stock photos. Scattered here and there are real pictures. My father and I smiling into the lens. Back before the Monster destroyed everything. A few of my Grandparents that I've never met and who died years ago.

It's sad, really. All this history lost. Lost to the Monster.

"All this is nothing anymore," I say as I walk up next to her.

Felicia looks at a picture of my dad and me, holding a fish on a hook. "What about this one? You're smiling."

"No," I say woodenly.

"Maybe you should keep it," Felicia says, fingering the worn framing around it. "Maybe one day you'll be able to use it move past all this."

"No. It's nothing now. Just one of those things I've lost. Besides, I'd rather not have him in my life anymore," I say with a nod the picture.

Felicia turns to me. "One of these days you'll have to face all this. You know that. Right?"

I sigh and my shoulders slump. "Yes," I say in agreement. "But I don't need his face staring at me every day."

"Do you have a picture of your mom?" she asks in a quiet, even tone.

"Not anymore."

Felicia nods and doesn't say anything else. I step out onto the porch, the cold sunlight clearing out the darkness. Eventually the Thompson's finish packing up the few boxes into the back of their truck. The pile is pitifully small and barely fills the bed. Felicia makes me set up an appointment to meet with her later in the week.

Before I get into Mrs. T's car, I turn to Alice and surprise her with a hug. "Thank you," I whisper.

"For what?"

"For protecting me while I was in there," I say, nodding at the house.

She looks at me a moment, before breaking into a big smile. "Anytime."

The Thompson's pull away from the curb. Brit and her father in the truck and me and Mrs. T in the car. Glancing back, I see Felicia and Alice watch us before turning away.

CHAPTER THIRTY-TWO

Moving in to the Thompson's takes less time than moving out of my old house. I feel bad making them hall my crap upstairs, but really, I'm not much use. Instead, I sit at the kitchen table and stare out the window, a steaming mug of coffee in my hand.

God, I really missed a good cup coffee while I was in the hospital. The crap they tried to feed me was beyond disgusting. Worse than anything I had at home. Well, the old house. This is home now. I know I should feel a sense of loss, but I can't. I'm too drained.

Brit walks in kisses me on the cheek. "Hey."

I smile up at her. "Hey."

"Please tell me that there is no cream or sugar in that," Brit says pointing to my coffee.

"Nope."

"Good," she says and steals a drink before sitting in the chair next to me.

"Hey!" I say, rescuing my coffee. "Get your own!"

Brit leans her elbows on the table and bats her eyelashes. I give her a flat look and slide my mug over to her. A triumphant grin spreads across her face and she and takes another drink before setting it back in front of me.

"We should give you a makeover," Brit announces.

"What?!"

"Seriously," she says without a trace a humor. "As hot as you are with the whole bad boy look, I want to give you a makeover. You know, a new look with a new start."

"Um, but I like my hair," I say sheepishly.

"Please?" Brit asks, giving me big doe eyes. Damn. I so want to kiss her right now.

"Fine," I reply with a mock glare. "But I'm not putting on makeup. Just the hair."

Brit giggles and rushes off for a pair of scissors and a comb before flouncing back into the room. I'm definitely going to regret this.

"Wait," I say, raising my hand for emphasis. "When did you learn to cut hair and why didn't I know this?"

Brit giggles again. "My mom taught me. She's been cutting our hair for years and finally showed me how."

I give Brit a worried look. "Um. I'm not so sure about this."

"Too late!" Brit cries and ties my hair up in a ponytail. "This would work better with clippers, but I don't have any. I'll have to fix it when I'm done."

Brit grabs my ponytail before I can escape.

"Ow!"

"Oh stop. You big baby!" She croons in my ear just before she kisses me on the neck, sending little jolts of electricity through my body. "Besides, you'll look sexier this way."

I blush and keep my mouth shut as she hacks through my hair. It takes a while and I end up with Mrs. T watching by the time she's done. She laughs and cheers Brit on as more and more of my hair falls to the floor. Each a piece of my soul, a part of my life before.

When Brit is finally done, she holds a mirror in front of me.

"It's not me." I'm not complaining. It's the truth. The person staring at me in the mirror is someone else. Someone I don't know. Someone who has survived a crucible of fire and lived to tell about it. His eyes are shadowed and full of pain and loss.

"I'm sorry," Brit says sadly.

"What?" It takes a second for my brain to make sense of what is going on. I'm a dick. She thinks I hate my hair.

"No," I say giving her hand a reassuring squeeze. "You did a good job. I just don't recognize myself anymore."

"You look like you," Brit says from the other side of the table. "You've just been through a lot lately. I'm sure you'll get used to it."

I shrug. "You're probably right."

The rest of the day is spent relaxing in front of the television with Brit snuggled up next to me. We can't be in my room alone, house rules, so we sit on the couch. Brit keeps playing with my hair and smiling at me. It's infectious and I'm smiling back. She makes me happy and I realize I really am happy. I know I have a lot of crap to deal with, but for the moment, life is good. I kiss her deeply, my tongue tracing her bottom lip. She shudders and opens her mouth, letting me in. I draw back and she pouts a little at the loss. God, she's hot.

"Thank you," I say as I gaze into her eyes.

"For what?" she asks, her cheeks turning pink.

"For being you."

Brit touches my face and kisses me a little deeper. We're interrupted by a polite cough as Mrs. T walks by and Brit and I grin at each other. It's a subtle warning. I will have to be careful, but we have plenty of time. We'll make it work.

Later that night when everyone is asleep, I pull out my sewing kit. It won't be easy with the splint and sore ribs, but I know now what to do with the blade. With a little luck, it won't take long. I look at the gleaming blade in my hand. It's such a small thing. I should throw it away, but it's a part of me. Like everything else on the jacket, it's a symbol of what has happened.

I use a small file and dull the edges. I have to be careful. The blade is really thin, and I don't want it to break. But leaving them alone might cause it to cut through the fabric. I do the best I can and wrap the edges in electrical tape just to make sure.

Once I finish that, I build it into the pocket using various folds and gaps. I've done it before on other parts of the jacket. I can insert hidden bits. Little mementos and such that I don't want anyone else to see. Pieces that are just for me and nobody else. Like the blade that almost ended everything. A part of me will always regret not doing it, but that, like everything else, is something I'll have to live with. Live. I never expected to do that, but I am.

I hide the remaining exposed section of the blade. It fits nicely over my heart, another hidden piece of armor. A small reminder of how close I came to ending it all. When I'm finished, my cheeks are damp with tears. I crawl into bed and hope that I don't dream about Lela, my father, or the other demons that plague my mind. One of these days I'll be free.

I try to go to sleep, but thinking of Brit down the hall sleeping keeps me awake. Eventually, I drift off. My dreams of Brit are interrupted by a warm body. Arms wrap around me and lips cover mine. I panic. Lela is back. In my half-awake state, I'm sure it is her. I push her away, trying to get free. My rational brain tries to claw its way to the forefront, but the panic is too deeply rooted.

Blinding light shocks me awake. Brit's concerned features come into focus and the here and now slams into my brain.

"Are you ok, Julius?"

I give her a weak smile and suppress a shudder as Lela is, once again, buried away with all my other pain and bad memories. Brit pulls me down against her, cradling my head in her arms. She murmurs soothing words into my ear as my body trembles with the residual fear. I curl up against her and let myself be weak for a moment. She won't judge.

"I'm so sorry, Jules. Whatever happened, I'm so sorry."

"Not your fault," I mumble into her shoulder, the tears finally drying up.

Her arms tighten around me. "Well, whatever happened, I'm here."

A part of me wants to tell her. Tell her about Lela. Blake should know the truth, but I can't talk to him. Everyone is still waiting for him to wake up. Nobody else knows the shame and fear that crushes me every time I think about her. I know it was the Monster that drove her to do it. She was scared, alone. I was understanding, a shoulder to cry on, a confidant. I didn't know what would happen. What she would take from me. I helped her escape my father so that I could escape her. When that didn't work, she left so I could be free.

Hot tears roll down my cheeks again, soaking the thin fabric of Brit's pajamas. She holds me and takes my pain. She doesn't ask for anything, she just holds me.

I pull away enough so that I can look at her. Her eyes are shining with tears. Tears for me and my pain. A part of me makes a decision, the rest of me is curled in a ball.

"Promise me," I say, hoping this is the right decision.

"What?" she asks.

"Promise me that you won't hate me."

A small smile plays across her lips and she strokes my cheek. "I couldn't hate you."

"Please." I need her to promise. I want to tell her everything, but I'm scared.

Brit kisses my nose. "I promise."

The words come haltingly, but I tell her. I tell her about the Monster. The one in my father and the one I'm scared is inside me. Most importantly, I tell her about Lela. Of what happened between us. Why she left. With each word, the weight lessons and I can breathe a little easier. Through it all, her hand gently strokes my cheek and she stares in my eyes. Showing me I'm not alone. When I'm done, she's crying for me and not because I hurt her.

At some point I fall asleep, cradled in her arms. For the first time, I don't dream about Lela or my father. I'm safe now.